"Don't be kind," Teddy told him in a voice that almost wasn't there.

Zach's mouth twisted as he bent toward her, murmuring, "I haven't got a kind bone in my body." He fitted his mouth to hers, firmly and with utter possession.

Instantly, Teddy responded, her arms going around his neck, a faint whimper escaping the molten joining of their lips. She could feel his hand slide around to the nape of her neck, drawing her up against him. Her body was pressed into the hardness of his chest, and the pleasure of that alone tightened an already quivering coil of desire deep inside her. They were locked together for long moments, and her body strained to be closer, to be a part of him.

He straightened up, and Teddy felt a flare of panic. "If you leave me now—"

Zach smiled slowly, his eyes never leaving hers. "No, honey, I'm not leaving you . . ."

Bantam Books by Kay Hooper

WHAT ARE *LOVESWEPT* ROMANCES?

They are stories of true romance and touching emotion. We believe those two very important ingredients are constants in our highly sensual and very believable stories in the *LOVESWEPT* line. Our goal is to give you, the reader, stories of consistently high quality that may sometimes make you laugh, sometimes make you cry, but are always fresh and creative and contain many delightful surprises within their pages.

Most romance fans read an enormous number of books. Those they truly love, they keep. Others may be traded with friends and soon forgotten. We hope that each *LOVESWEPT* romance will be a treasure—a "keeper." We will always try to publish

LOVE STORIES YOU'LL NEVER FORGET
BY AUTHORS YOU'LL ALWAYS REMEMBER

The Editors

LOVESWEPT® • 225

Kay Hooper
Zach's Law

BANTAM BOOKS
TORONTO • NEW YORK • LONDON • SYDNEY • AUCKLAND

ZACH'S LAW

A Bantam Book / December 1987

LOVESWEPT® and the wave device are registered trademarks of Bantam Books, Inc. Registered in U.S. Patent and Trademark Office and elsewhere.

If you would be interested in receiving protective vinyl covers for your Loveswept books, please write to this address for information:

Loveswept
Bantam Books
P.O. Box 985
Hicksville, NY 11802

ISBN 0-553-21852-2

Published simultaneously in the United States and Canada

Bantam Books are published by Bantam Books, Inc. Its trademark, consisting of the words "Bantam Books" and the portrayal of a rooster, is Registered in U.S. Patent and Trademark Office and in other countries. Marca Registrada. Bantam Books, Inc., 666 Fifth Avenue, New York, New York 10103.

PRINTED IN THE UNITED STATES OF AMERICA

O   0 9 8 7 6 5 4 3 2 1

for Eileen—
thanks

"Now this is the Law of the Jungle—
as old and as true as the sky;
And the Wolf that shall keep it may prosper,
but the Wolf that shall break it must die."

—Kipling

One

Theodora Suzanne Jessica Tyler realized she'd made a mistake. Not a big one, really, except that it now looked as though she'd landed herself in a first-class *mess*. She was miles away from civilization, it was after midnight, and her beloved old Impala had just given up the ghost.

Swearing, Teddy got out of the car and slammed the door, annoyed at herself rather than the Impala. She'd been warned, after all, that the car probably wouldn't be able to stand the trip across the Rockies. And the poor thing had groaned and wheezed when she'd started the engine hours ago in that little town.

"So what if their only hotel was a crummy one?" she told the car in disgust. "At least it had a roof. And there was a telephone. I could have put you in for repairs in that garage for a couple of days. I *should* have. Then we wouldn't be stuck halfway down a mountain and miles from everything." She glanced around at total darkness, adding a bit louder, "And on a deserted road, dammit. Except for us, there's been no traffic for fifty miles."

Dispiritedly, she kicked a tire gently and began to swear in a steady voice. It made her feel better. Her voice was a rational sound in the utter quiet of a deserted night, and comforting for that reason.

Teddy was accustomed to being alone, but she didn't like being *this* alone. And since panic was alien to her nature, she began to get angrier.

"There must be somebody in this godforsaken wilderness. Maybe if I blew the horn—"

There was somebody in the wilderness.

When he reached out, the last thing Zach expected to gather to his massive chest was a small, soft, decidedly feminine armful with a fine talent for creative cursing and great survival instincts. He'd heard a woman speak, but she'd sounded *taller* somehow, and it was too dark to see clearly.

He clamped one big hand over her mouth, cutting off the loud and colorful swearing, and tried not to hurt her while also trying to protect vulnerable parts of his anatomy from her rage.

"Hold it!" he growled hastily. "I'm not going to hurt you!"

She chose not to believe him. She also chose to bring her small, booted heel down squarely on his left foot, and since he wasn't wearing boots himself, the contact was definitely painful. She also bit him.

"Dammit!" He grunted with pain, shifting his feet and momentarily releasing her mouth.

"Let go of me, you big oaf!" she said, then drew a deep breath.

Since he couldn't afford to let her scream, Zach

covered her mouth again. Her response was a series of indignant kicks and a few violent and improbable wiggles. A bit indignant himself, he lifted her completely off her feet and tightened his grasp with the care of a large and powerful man who knew his own vast strength to the last ounce; he was still hoping he wouldn't hurt her.

Speaking in a soft voice near her ear, he said, "I'll uncover your mouth if you won't scream—and if you *do* scream, I swear I'll deck a woman for the first time in my life!"

She bit him again.

Hampered by having to hold her and desperately determined that she make no sound, Zach briefly considered his options. They weren't promising. The last thing he wanted to do was knock her out. She was reacting fairly reasonably to her situation as she saw it, and had done nothing to deserve a forced nap. Besides, if Zach had any soft spot at all, it was for little women with more courage and temper than sense. Like her.

"I *won't* hurt you," he repeated, switching to a soothing tone and managing to set her on her feet just long enough to pull a handkerchief from his pocket. Before she could start kicking again, he distracted her by removing his hand from her mouth and quickly replacing it with the handkerchief. He had her gagged in just a few seconds and had her back off her feet before she could give vent to her renewed rage.

The sounds she made now were muffled and unintelligible, which was all he could hope for; he was silently praying the noises reached no more than a few yards in any direction. He had to work quickly and quietly, and his mind was racing over those few options.

He couldn't let her go even if he could get the car running again. In her mood, she was sure to drive straight to the nearest town—a scant ten miles away—and report her encounter with a murderous fiend on the roadside. Even if he could explain his behavior, which he couldn't, he didn't dare attract attention. He couldn't tie her up and leave her in the car; if anyone found her, it would likely be the wrong people. And if he kept her with him, she was sure as hell going to prove a royal pain in the rear— whether or not he could convince her he was on the side of the angels.

Lousy options.

Swearing softly and being unconsciously fierce about it, Zach finally managed to wrestle her over to a slender tree and used his belt to bind her wrists together behind it. Then, ignoring the blue-tinted noises coming from behind the gag, he approached the car and used his pencil flashlight to check it out. The rusting Impala was over twenty years old; it didn't take Zach five minutes to realize the car had died and that its resurrection depended on nothing less than a new engine.

He stood beside it for a moment, gazing thoughtfully in the dark down the straight stretch of road. Finally, with a philosophical shrug, he reached inside and got the keys. The unlocked trunk revealed a couple of swollen suitcases, which he retrieved and put by the side of the road. Then he got in and methodically went through the car, gathering every shred of paper he could find and stuffing them into the pocket of his flannel jacket.

There was a large leather handbag inside, as well

as a thermos and a tote bag filled with various snacks, and he put those by the side of the road. Just to be sure, he also searched beneath the seats and under the floor mats. He found a roll of electrician's tape in the glove compartment and used that to lock the steering wheel in place, then knocked the car out of gear and released the emergency brake.

He got out and went around to the rear of the car, standing still for a long moment as he listened. Sound carried in the mountains, and he knew he'd hear if another car was within miles. There was no sound. Bending, he pushed hard, his considerable muscles bunching with the effort. The car began rolling, and thirty seconds later Zach watched the last faint glint of it disappear silently into the darkness.

This stretch of road ended, he knew, in a gentle curve overlooking a small lake. The car wouldn't make the turn. Several minutes passed before Zach heard the distant splash of something heavy finishing off a high dive into the lake in grand style.

A muffled wail came from behind him, and Zach sighed as he loaded up the woman's stuff and carried it into the woods. It didn't take long to get the bags to his place. Minutes later, he was back at the tree, gazing at her. Despite highly developed night vision, he couldn't see much, but judging by her movements, the lady was still furious.

He couldn't really blame her.

He was more worried at the moment, however, by their proximity to the house. He glanced in that direction, relieved to find no light shining through the trees. With any luck at all, he decided, they hadn't made enough commotion to attract attention.

Wondering what in heaven's name he was going

to do with her, Zach unfastened the lady's wrists, avoiding her kicking and managing to get her away from the tree. He bound her wrists behind her back again, then hoisted her easily over one shoulder. It was simple to hold both her tiny ankles and prevent her from kicking him, but her struggles slightly upset his balance. He slapped her smartly on the rear with his free hand, muttering softly, "Be still!" Not that she did; an indignant note was now added to the furious sounds still emanating from behind the gag.

He carried her through the woods and away from the house and road. Within moments they were deep into the forest. Zach could move quickly and quietly, especially for a man of his size and weight. He slowed at last, pushing his way through a tangle of undergrowth, ivy, and brambles that hid a small rickety cabin. He opened the surprisingly well-fitted door and carried her inside, closing the door behind them.

It was pitch dark inside, but he moved unerringly across the small room and dropped her gently onto a wide, sturdy cot. Then he double-checked to make certain the heavy shades still guarded the two small windows before he turned on a large, battery-powered lamp. The light was strong, and Zach turned with a great many misgivings to contemplate his unexpected—and unwelcome—guest.

The first thing he noticed was her hair. There seemed to be a great deal of it for so tiny a woman, and it was such a bright red as to seem unreal. Above the strip of white linen guarding her mouth was a delicate nose sprinkled with freckles and large, spaniel-brown eyes. Her eyes dominated her face, giving her a waiflike appearance. Her skin was the creamy white of a true redhead, and though she was certainly a small woman, Zach knew there were quite a few eye-catching curves beneath her heavy sweater and jeans. He'd felt them.

She wasn't beautiful, but there was something endearingly sweet and fresh about her face. Cute. She was cute, he decided judiciously. She was also, he realized, staring at him in alarm. Fear.

He didn't have to ask what had altered the rage to fear even as he'd turned to face her. The scar. He never quite forgot he bore that scar, even though he wasn't self-conscious about it. The thin silver mark ran from the corner of his left eye to his jaw, and though it wasn't disfiguring, he knew it lent his face a look of menace, perhaps even cruelty.

Especially in a situation like this.

Zach sighed a little and moved to sit on the edge of the cot. She didn't shrink away from him, but he could feel her stiffen. He untied the gag, then released her wrists. He spoke finally, keeping his voice even and calm.

"I said I wouldn't hurt you, and I meant that. But you've stumbled into something dangerous, and I can't let you go until it's all over." He glanced down to watch her massaging her wrists, and felt a pang of regret when he saw the red marks that the belt had left on her white skin.

Frowning a little, he got up again and went over to unearth a first-aid kit from a cluttered shelf by the door. He opened the kit and found a tube of salve, then carried it back to the cot and sat down again. "Here—" He reached for her wrist.

Instantly, she drew away from him until her back was against the wall. And for someone who'd sworn steadily for so long, she was surprisingly silent now.

Zach's face settled into its habitual bland expression. He dropped the tube onto the blanket at her side. "Use that on your wrists," he said impersonally. "It's a commercial first-aid cream." He rose and went over to where her bags were piled under one window, picking up the thermos. Finding reasonably hot coffee inside, he poured some into the plastic cup and carried it to her. "It's your coffee," he reminded, still impersonal. "And you may have noticed I neither drugged nor poisoned it."

After a moment she sat up and gingerly took the cup from his outstretched hand.

Zach watched her sip the liquid, still bothered both by her red wrists and the wary alarm in her eyes. "You don't have to be afraid of me," he said finally in a softened tone. "I'd let you go right now, but it could be dangerous for you. And don't let the scar fool you—I'm not as mean as I look."

Her eyes flickered, and her gaze slid away from his to stare at his cheek. She seemed surprised. And she sounded both surprised and curiously annoyed when she finally spoke.

"I didn't even notice that. It's hardly visible." Her voice, robbed of the fire and brimstone, was musical, faintly husky.

Zach was surprised. "Then why did you suddenly look afraid when I turned to face you?"

She pointed at him and grimaced. "That."

He looked down and saw that his flannel jacket had fallen open to reveal the gun he wore in a shoulder holster. "Oh." He looked back at her, smiling a little. "I'd forgotten."

She continued to look wary, but something seemed to have eased her mind. "How could you forget a gun that big?"

"You get used to it."

After a moment she said in a small voice, "Tell me you're a cop."

"Sorry."

"No badge?"

"No badge."

"But you aren't going to hurt me?"

"I swear."

Her gaze wandered around the room, settling on the jumble of electronic equipment weighing down a makeshift counter. She recognized what looked like a portable computer, but there was nothing else she could identify. She thought vaguely that the square things on the floor could be batteries. Maybe. And there was something that might have been a radio, complete with headphones.

The remainder of the room was also filled with equipment—and other things. There were two rifles propped against a wall, with boxes of ammunition stacked beside them. There was a small refrigerator and a butane stove and some kind of heater that whirred softly. Open shelves revealed canned goods and other foodstuffs, along with stacks of paper plates and plastic cups and utensils. The battery-powered lamp sat on a small wooden table boasting two sturdy looking chairs. There was a sink with an old manual pump, and there was the bed she sat on.

It looked like this man had been here for a while. And that he was ready for just about anything, including a siege.

Teddy looked back at him finally, trying to weigh her various impressions. He was definitely an intimidating man, partly because of his sheer size and the raw power he exuded. His voice was soft and effortless, and his gray eyes were serene—deceptively so, she thought. And though that rugged face was bland, it was also hard.

What on earth had she stumbled into?

"Why would it be dangerous for me if you let me go?"

"It's ten miles to the nearest town."

Teddy was frowning a little, working only on instinct as she tried to read his expressionless face. "That isn't what you meant."

Zach had been prepared for a kind of "prisoner of war" reaction from her, something he was familiar with. He'd expected a logical progression in her reactions to being held against her will. First, the frightened silence and suspicion of his every move. Then nervous questions and promises that she wouldn't tell anyone about him. When that didn't work, she'd be quiescent for a while before attempting to escape. Failing to escape, she'd be enraged and frustrated by helplessness.

And if he was forced to keep her prisoner long enough, her reaction would be one that would make him despise himself. There would be a gradual progression to shock, apathy. There would also come a time when she would likely develop a sort of emotional dependence on him; he had seen it happen. And that final response could easily leave more scars on the "kidnapper" than the victim.

He had known that to happen too.

Zach didn't want any of those things to take place. And he was somewhat encouraged because after her first rational fear passed, she seemed more curious and thoughtful than anxious. It would, he knew, be greatly to her benefit if she could accept the situation calmly and feel relatively unthreatened by it. If he could keep his own attitude low-key and reasonable, maybe they'd both get out of this all right. Maybe.

Now those shrewd brown eyes waited for a response, and Zach weighed his words carefully. "That was partly what I meant," he said slowly.

"But there was more to it." She glanced around the room, then back at him. "What're you doing up here?"

Zach had never been one to trust easily and so he didn't answer, but merely said, "Put some first-aid cream on your wrists."

After a moment she set her cup aside and picked up the tube. Rubbing the cream into her bruised and chafed flesh, she asked, "How long do you expect to keep me here?"

Zach was pouring himself a cup of coffee from the pot on the small stove. "No longer than necessary."

Her eyes followed him as he sat in a chair by the table. "Then you'll turn me loose? You drowned my car," she reminded him. "How will I get out of here?"

He shrugged. "I'll take you to a town."

"You have a car up here?"

He smiled faintly. "No."

Teddy abandoned the possibility of stealing his car. "Well, dammit," she muttered. The amusement in his eyes irritated her, and she went on aggrievedly, "If you *were* a cop, I could probably get a new car out of this. You know, official appeasement of a defenseless woman attacked on the roadside by a cop who subsequently trashed her car."

He shrugged again, still amused. "You car was already dead. I just buried it."

She stared at him. "D'you have a name?"

"Zach Steele." If she got away, he decided, it was

all over, anyway—her knowing his name wouldn't matter.

"At least you didn't say John Smith."

"I'm a very truthful man. What's your name?"

"Theodora Suzanne Jessica Tyler." She said it with a trace of defiance that was almost automatic.

He blinked. "Quite a handle. Is there a shortened version?"

"Teddy."

Zach liked that; it suited her, he thought. But all he said was, "I have to do some work, Teddy—mostly inside this cabin. A day, maybe two. I don't want to have to tie you up or gag you again, but you'll have to be quiet. And even if you get outside, you won't know where you are. You could easily get lost."

Teddy was slowly recapping the tube of salve and looking at him thoughtfully. "Or I could run into someone who *is* meaner than he looks?"

He was a little surprised and wondered if she was simply guessing. "Why do you say that?"

Obviously annoyed, she said, "I'm not blind." She nodded toward the rifles and ammunition. "As I understand it, the game up here doesn't shoot back. And then there's your handgun—hardly standard hunting equipment. Unless you're hunting something that walks on two legs and *does* shoot back. Stop me if I'm getting warm."

"Stop," he murmured.

"I don't suppose you're a modern-day bounty hunter?"

"No."

"Good. The kind of cop that doesn't carry a badge, maybe?"

"What kind is that?" he asked neutrally.

She studied him. "Oh . . . one who's undercover.

A federal cop, maybe. Or one who's on a stakeout. That's equipment designed to listen in on something," she added with a nod toward the electronic jumble.

Zach returned her stare, his own growing unconsciously harder, suspicious. "Just where were you headed when your car died?" he asked.

Teddy couldn't help swallowing hard, though she managed not to look away from his suddenly icy gray eyes. "Not around here, that's for sure. I was heading back East to visit relatives."

"I don't suppose you can prove that?"

Her chin lifted, and her own eyes grew stormy. "No. I don't suppose I can."

After a moment Zach reached into his pocket and began pulling out the papers he'd gotten from her car. He looked through them carefully, all the while keeping an unobtrusive eye on her. She didn't stir, but those brown eyes were still stormy.

The papers were the innocent ones found in most cars. A registration slip in her name. A few road maps: California, Nevada, Utah, Colorado. Three years' worth of inspection slips. Four tattered shopping lists, half a dozen crumpled receipts tangled with green stamps, a dusty mileage log filled with entries and bearing both her name and an unreadably smeared official looking stamp inside the front cover.

Zach looked at her for a moment, then reached out a long arm to snag the big leather purse. She never changed expression, but Zach nonetheless hesitated. There was something so damned *personal* about a woman's purse, he thought, and he felt ridiculously in the wrong about rummaging through it. Then, to his surprise, he caught a sardonic gleam in her eyes, and she gestured slightly.

"Go ahead."

He had to be certain she wasn't involved in this; there was too much at stake. Accordingly, Zach opened the purse. Three seconds later he understood her faint mockery. And since he had never in his life opened a woman's purse, he had to wonder in astonishment if Teddy's was par for the course.

The pocket calendar made sense, he thought, as did the hairbrush, compact, and lipstick. He lifted these out carefully and set them on the table. Then, one bit at a time, he lifted out the rest. There was a flimsy string bag, bunched in a knot. There was an overlarge, decidedly bulky leather work-glove—left-handed. There was a small notebook with lined blank pages and three pens clipped to it. There was a dog leash designed to restrain anything up to and including a rabid St. Bernard. There was a folding leather case holding a selection of darts and a small vial of liquid labeled "tranquilizer."

Somewhat thoughtfully, Zach buttoned that into his pocket.

There was an electric bill, stamped paid, a phone bill, also stamped, an address book, two packages of chewing gum, a book of postage stamps, a long silk scarf, a braided leather belt, a toothbrush in a plastic case, a small penknife, a large and crowded ring of keys, a contact lens case, a much-handled deck of playing cards, one pair of sunglasses, and one pair of dark-rimmed corrective lenses—both in cases.

In the very bottom of the purse, lying in a nest of coins, paper clips, and rubber bands, was a leather billfold. Zach drew that out and opened it. He didn't bother to check for cash but looked instead for identification. Behind the plastic sleeve containing a picture of Teddy on an elephant were other sleeves holding credit cards, a donor card, a California driver's license, a social security card, several business cards, and an identity card naming Teddy as an Animal Control Officer for the city of San Francisco.

"Can I go through your pockets now?" she asked politely.

Zach replaced everything in the purse, then drew out his wallet and tossed it to her in silence.

She was obviously surprised, but that didn't stop her from opening the wallet and looking through it. She, too, ignored cash for other things. She found several credit cards—including two major ones authorized to Zach but in the name of a company she recognized, partly because it was constantly in the news.

"Long Enterprises." She looked at him quickly. "Joshua Long's company? You work for him?"

Zach made a silent mental note to tell Josh he was getting too damned well-known outside business circles—as if he hadn't always been famous. Or infamous. "Yes. But I'm presently on vacation."

After a moment Teddy went back to examining the wallet. A New York driver's license. Social security card. A permit to carry a concealed weapon. Identification naming Zach as a security consultant. A donor card. No photos.

Teddy closed the wallet and tossed it back to him. Detached, she said, "We both know any of this stuff could have been faked. So where did it get us?"

"I believe you were just passing through," he told her.

She was curious. "What convinced you?"

"I think it was the dog leash."

Teddy blinked. "Oh. And what am I supposed to believe?"

Zach looked at her and quite suddenly wished they were in another place at another time. "Whatever you want to believe, I guess."

She finished her coffee in silence and set the cup aside, trying to read his bland, hard face. It was impossible. His expression was unnerving—but not frightening. Not really. She felt peculiarly safe with this stranger.

"How long?" she asked abruptly. "You must have some idea."

"A week, if we're lucky."

"And if we aren't?"

"Then it'll be longer."

Teddy drew a soft breath. "And if I told you that my sister is expecting a call tomorrow to let her know I'm all right?"

"I'm sorry," he said sincerely.

She bit her lip. "Look, my sister is five months' pregnant, and she's miscarried twice. She knows the car isn't—wasn't—running too well. If I don't let her know I'm okay, she's going to worry."

Zach gazed into those pleading eyes and wished for the second time that they were somewhere else. After a moment he sighed himself. "I'll think of something. For now, why don't you get some sleep?"

"I'm not sleepy."

He sat back and sipped his coffee, watching her.

Teddy stirred restlessly. In a tone of foreboding she said, "If you're the strong and silent type, we're in trouble. I'm a talker. Silence drives me crazy." She stared at him, adding sardonically, "Don't tell me, loose lips sink ships?"

"Well, they do." His tone was mild. "As it happens, though, I just don't have anything to say."

"The situation's getting worse. All right, accepting—

not that I do—the fact that we're not going to discuss what you're doing here, there must be some
safe topic. Ummm . . . let's talk about your famous
employer. Or is he involved in this thing you're doing?
No, you wouldn't answer that, would—"

"He's not involved," Zach interrupted firmly. "I
told you, I'm on vacation."

"Then let's talk about him." Teddy clasped her
arms around her upraised knees and leaned back
against the wall. "The press has been going hot and
heavy for months over the possibility that Long has
gotten involved with that island dictator. They seem
to think he's about to invest in President Sereno's
country."

Zach remained impassive.

Teddy eyed him. "We're not going to talk about
that?"

"I'm not."

"It violates national security, I suppose?"

He said nothing.

With a sigh Teddy said, "You're worse than a clam.
What *can* we talk about? The weather requires no
discussion, and things like politics drive me nuts.
What does a security consultant do?" she asked
abruptly.

Zach shrugged. "Consults. Checks out security
systems, designs and installs them, solves security
problems."

"You do that for Long Enterprises?"

"Yes."

Her gaze wandered around the room, focusing on
the computer. "You work with computers?"

"Yes."

"I mean, *really* work with them? Program them
and stuff like that?"

"Yes."

Quite suddenly, Teddy snatched up her empty plastic coffee cup and threw it at him. Zach deflected the missile with the quick instinctive reflexes of a fighter and stared at her stormy face in surprise.

"Did I miss something?" he asked dryly.

Her only response to the question was a deepening of her glare. "A clam. You'd make a lousy talk-show guest, you know that? One-word answers! Instruct the witness to answer just yes or no, please, Your Honor. We don't want to waste the court's time."

Zach, who had never gone in much for small talk or social conversation, shrugged somewhat helplessly. "Sorry."

Teddy rested her forehead on her upraised knees, and her voice emerged muffled. "I can see this is going to be a *long* incarceration."

She awoke to faint jingling sounds and sat up, rubbing her eyes sleepily and blinking away the morning dryness of her contact lenses. When she could focus, she saw Zach unbuckling a tool belt from around his waist, and watched while he sat down and began removing spiked boots from both feet.

"Have you been climbing telephone poles?" she asked in a voice still thick with sleep. It was then that she realized he'd been out of the cabin and that she could have escaped. Her disappointment was mild, which surprised her.

"You wanted to let your sister know you were all right," he reminded her, hanging his coat on a peg by the door and going over to sit before the computer.

Teddy pushed away the blankets, wondering if he had covered her and removed her boots after she'd fallen asleep; she couldn't even remember falling asleep. "Yes, but there's no phone. Is there?"

"Next best thing," he murmured, turning on the computer.

She got to her feet, stretching, and padded over to stand beside him. She was only partially awake but was still able to understand what he was doing. Access codes. He was using a connection to the phone lines to communicate with another computer. Teddy opened her mouth to comment, then decided there was no earthly reason why this large man should know the extent of her own knowledge.

"What're you doing?"

"Leaving a message," he answered absently, still typing.

"My sister doesn't have a computer."

"Long Enterprises does."

Two

A gleaming high rise in New York City housed the "home base" of Long Enterprises, and the entire fifteenth floor contained what was, in essence, the technological brain of the organization. Every room and office held a computer console, each tied to the central data base that Zach Steele had designed. Every worker could request data from the central bank, but various security systems and access codes prevented anyone from gaining access to anything restricted without the proper permission. And only those with top clearance could use computers to call "outside" the system through the telephone lines and via a modem—a practice that even with every precaution taken could leave the system open to tampering.

Lucas Kendrick, as chief investigator for the company, was one of the few with a top clearance, and he sat now in his office, yawning and drinking coffee, while he watched the blank screen of his humming console. His silvery blond hair bore the appearance of having had fingers run through it several times, and his blue eyes, though sharp, were also a bit sleepy.

It was just before eight A.M. New York time, on a mild Tuesday morning.

"Anything?" Rafferty Lewis came in and rested a hip on the corner of Lucas's desk, holding a cup of coffee and, like Lucas, looking as if he'd been awakened rudely and before he was ready to face the day.

"Nothing yet." Lucas checked his watch. "Should be coming through shortly, though."

"Any idea where he is?" Rafferty asked him, impatiently brushing back a lock of coppery hair that insisted on falling over his forehead.

Lucas shook his head. "I only know what I told you over the phone. Tracy was working in the central computer room as usual last night, and she called me because when she checked the mainframe, there was a message flag. Zach wanted me to stand by this morning, leaving my console on-line." His voice was low and curiously compelling, a voice that could charm the devil out of hell.

"I don't suppose we could trace the call?" Rafferty's lazy voice successfully hid the fact that he was one of Harvard Law School's more brilliant graduates—something various courtroom opponents had discovered at their cost.

"From Zach? No way. He'll probably have the call routed through so many dead ends that we wouldn't be able to trace it if we had a month."

Rafferty looked at his friend thoughtfully. "Is that why you called me? Because he's covering his tracks?"

"Something's up. And I have this hollow feeling that it has to do with our federal nemesis."

"Hagen?" Rafferty frowned. "We haven't heard from him in months, not since Kadeira."

Lucas grunted. "Want to bet he's found some *assignment* that just cries out for a man of Zach's vast talents?"

"I wouldn't waste my money. I do wonder how he managed to convince Zach, though. Josh and Raven won't be back for another week, right?" He waited for the nod. "I'll call Sarah a little later and see if she can find out anything. She's the only one of us in a position to get quick information, since she still works for him."

Lucas looked up at him; he seemed especially solemn. "How's the mother-to-be doing? Is she still serving you crackers in bed every morning?"

"Shut up," Rafferty told him politely, but he took a hasty sip of coffee as if to ward off nausea. Then, aggrievedly, he added, "I don't care if it *is* a common phenomenon, I could sure do without it. Sarah bounds out of bed looking radiant every morning and eats anything she wants, and I walk around looking like a corpse."

Lucas eyed him. "Uh-huh."

There was no opportunity for Rafferty to retort, since the computer beeped just then, demanding attention.

"It's coming through now," Lucas said, humor fleeing.

Rafferty leaned forward to watch the screen, serious as well. "About time."

Teddy was hardly aware her forearm was resting on Zach's broad shoulder as she leaned forward to watch intently. Never very appearance-conscious, she was unconcerned that she had slept in her clothes, that her hair hadn't been brushed this morning, and that she wore no makeup. And if she'd been told that she looked glorious this morning, she would have been amused and disbelieving.

Zach had almost said as much to her. After the first contact well before dawn, Zach had waited to give Lucas time to get to the computer in New York. He had been silent, Teddy had been half asleep, so they had said very little to each other.

Now they could get a message through. She spelled her sister's married name for him and watched the silent conversation on the screen continue, commenting only, "Isn't it illegal to use language like that through the telephone lines?"

Trying to ignore her nearness and the elusive scent that reminded him of a mountain meadow in spring, he said, "Lucas isn't happy with me, I'm afraid."

"Obviously." She watched a moment longer. " 'Just because the boss is in Canada'—who's the boss? Long?"

"Um." Zach quickly typed a response to Lucas's reprimand.

"Have permission, do you?" Teddy murmured, watching words appear on the screen. Then she added, "I don't think your friend is buying that."

Zach typed a final decisive sentence, then turned the computer off before Lucas could berate him anymore.

"Will he deliver the message to Jennifer?" Teddy asked, straightening as she abruptly reminded herself this man was still wearing a gun.

"He'll deliver it. And he has the charm to reassure her that you're fine."

Teddy hastily removed her arm from his shoulder. "Oh. Good." She looked around, spotting a narrow door at the back of the cabin. "That wouldn't happen to be a bathroom, would it?"

"It would, such as it is."

She went to check out the room, looking around the doorjamb a moment later to say resignedly, "There's no shower or tub."

"Sorry. There's a stream not too far away."

Teddy looked at him with the obvious horror of a city girl asked to do the unthinkable. "You mean you bathe in a freezing mountain stream?"

"Sure."

She shivered elaborately, muttered, "No way," and vanished back into the tiny room, closing the door behind her.

Zach wasn't worried she'd escape; there was no window in there. Besides, he had a feeling he could leave the front door wide open and she wouldn't try to get away. Not in her current mood, at any rate. She had fallen asleep last night with the suddenness of a child and slept deeply until morning. An unconscious sign of trust, he thought. And she had certainly accepted him to the extent of leaning on him companionably for long minutes while watching him work at the computer.

It had been unconscious, and he had shrewdly noted the moment she'd become aware of her action and had somewhat hastily withdrawn from that closeness. Zach looked down at the large hands resting on either side of the keyboard, and his jaw tightened.

With a movement that was almost savage, he turned the computer back on. Useless, he thought, to wish again they'd met in another place and time.

And useless to hope this entire situation turned out happily for all concerned.

Zach didn't believe in fairy-tale endings.

He was busy working at the console when she came out of the bathroom to get a few things from her suitcase, so Teddy didn't disturb him. She dug out a change of clothes, her toothbrush and toilet articles, then returned to the bathroom and did the best she could to freshen up.

Her movements were automatic, and she hardly looked at her reflection in the cracked mirror above the bare porcelain sink. She was thinking, and since she was surprisingly logical for so emotional a woman, she was listing her conclusions mentally.

She believed Zach Steele wouldn't hurt her. She had gone to sleep naturally in his presence, which meant she instinctively trusted him. He had gone out of his way to find some means of contacting her sister to provide reassurance—granted, though, that could have been merely because he didn't want an alarm raised.

Teddy was intrigued. She stopped brushing her unruly hair and gazed blindly into the mirror. She had dreamed about Zach. And the dream had left her with a feeling of safety and security—but there had also been a peculiar excitement and an unfamiliar, vivid awareness of the man.

He certainly wasn't a man one could ignore.

And her reaction to him was . . . confusing. It was a combination of three separate responses. Intellectually, she was intrigued by the puzzle of what he was up to and frustrated by how taciturn he was; physically, she was highly conscious of the raw, almost animal virility of his big body; and emotionally—what? Emotionally, she was powerfully drawn to him.

Why? *Why*? What had happened during their brief hours together that had destroyed her fear and created these other feelings?

Had it been because the marks on her wrists had obviously disturbed him? Because he had hesitated to look into her purse? Because he had seemed to believe almost automatically that the faint scar on his face had frightened her? Because there were no pictures, no indications of his past or personality in his wallet?

Teddy swore quietly and set her brush aside. She looked into the cracked mirror, really looked, and the slightly distorted reflection of her face was disquieting.

She didn't recognize herself.

When she went back into the main room of the cabin, he was still working at the computer. Keeping her distance from him, she asked tentatively, "I don't suppose I can watch what you're doing?"

"I'd rather you didn't," he answered immediately, without turning around.

"Well, then, d'you mind if I do something about breakfast?"

"No, go ahead." He glanced around at her then, and for an instant there was a flicker of humor in his gray eyes. "When this is over, you can write a book about being held hostage and forced to cook your own breakfast."

"Don't think I don't appreciate the irony of the situation," she told him, walking over to study the small stove and shelf of canned and dry goods. Continuing absently, she said, "I guess I could make things harder on us both, but that idea doesn't appeal to me much. By the way—why is there only a pump out here but a regular faucet in the bathroom?"

"Beats me. I think this used to be a hunter's cabin, built twenty or thirty years ago from the look of it. The bathroom is a recent addition. I suppose there could have been some idea of turning this place into a guest cottage or something when the house was built—" He broke off abruptly, a mixture of surprise and irritation flashing briefly across his face.

Teddy looked at him but didn't ask the natural question, "What house?" Instead, she said merely, "Oh. Any preference as to breakfast?"

"Suit yourself." He returned his attention to the computer, still annoyed with himself for mentioning the house. Behind him, Teddy worked quietly, humming all the while. Zach found himself thinking of what a lovely voice she had, and his irritation grew. He frowned at the screen, absorbing the detailed descriptions of a dozen paintings, four necklaces, six rings, and a score of unset gemstones that had been stolen the previous week.

"Interpol?" she exclaimed from just behind him.

Zach turned quickly.

"All right, I snooped," she agreed hastily, "but I couldn't help it." She was standing a foot away, her eyes flickering from his face to the computer screen. "Interpol has a computer? I didn't know that. I guess they'd have to, though, wouldn't they? I mean, since they're an international organization?" She was babbling nervously and knew it. There was something about the expression on Zach's face that unnerved her.

"Shut it off," he said softly.

Instantly, she did, falling silent and staring at him.

Zach drew a deep breath, holding her gaze steadily. "Look, I know you didn't ask to get mixed up in this, but the fact remains that you're stuck here for the duration. How long that'll be depends on several factors beyond my control, but you can help shorten the time by leaving me alone to do what I have to— and by not asking questions. I know you're curious, I know that's natural, but I simply can't afford to satisfy your curiosity. And, to be blunt, it'll be better for you to know as little as possible. Now, if you can't live with that, I'll have to waste a hell of a lot of valuable time and probably ruin weeks of work by getting you out of here and having a friend of mine keep you under house arrest somewhere until I've finished what I came here to do. Understand?"

It was the most she'd heard him say, but it was the faint chill in his gray eyes and the snap to his voice that had the stronger effect. She nodded, then went back to her work at the stove, utterly silent.

Zach ran the fingers of his right hand through his thick black hair, unsettled by his own display of temper. He was rarely irritable; his anger, when it was roused at all, took the form of usually violent action with little words.

He gazed at her slender, stiff back, wondering what had happened to his intentions of being low-key and reasonable. Even though his reasoning had been accurate, he hadn't meant to scare her. He could hardly fault her for having no idea what she'd stumbled into, and it *was* perfectly natural for her to be curious.

And he just might have wrecked even her unconscious trust in him—which he didn't know how he'd earned in the first place—and put them right back where they'd started.

He hesitated only a moment, then rose and moved to stand just behind her. "Teddy? I'm sorry, I didn't mean to snap at you."

She had made a batter from flour and thinned evaporated milk, and was preparing pancakes. She didn't turn to face him. "You were right, it isn't any of my business. I'm just the hostage." Her voice wasn't meek or frightened—it was tight and furious.

Zach was almost relieved but also wary. He was certain her spirited temperament would see her through this with a minimum of emotional scars, but it seemed likely that he'd find a few new marks on his own hide before they were through.

He responded carefully. "The door's unlocked, and I neither tied you up nor locked the door when I left earlier to patch into the phone lines. I'm trusting you, Teddy."

Some of the stiffness left her shoulders, but she didn't turn around. "Sure you are," she said sardonically.

He reached over her to set the pan off the burner, then turned her around, his hands on her shoulders, dimly surprised that he was so intent on convincing her. "Teddy . . ." His voice deepened and a fierce note entered it. "If the timing weren't so critical, I'd get you out of here, someplace safe. But I can't afford to leave. And that means you have to stay here and do as I say."

Eyes stormy, she said, "So I have to accept blindly and follow orders? If that's the kind of macho crap you're used to, pal, you're in for a sur—"

He shook her, hard. "It's got nothing to do with being macho, dammit!" he growled. "It concerns keeping your pretty little butt out of one hell of a dangerous sling!"

"That's right," she mockingly, "scare the poor silly woman to keep her quiet and obedient! Just what century did you grow up in, anyway? I can take care of myself, dammit. I don't need some overgrown, overbearing, arrogant, son of a sexist *dog* telling me what to do!" She was almost shouting on the last words, angrier than she could ever remember being and not exactly sure why, especially since she wasn't a feminist and knew perfectly well that he wasn't being sexist.

It was very puzzling.

When she drew a breath to continue her tirade, Zach muttered, "Ahhh—*hell!*" and used a rather old, timeworn, and arguably sexist solution to the problem of her noisy defiance: He kissed her.

Teddy found herself lifted completely off her feet and held against his massive chest in an immensely disconcerting bear hug. It wasn't painful, but her senses hadn't suffered a shock like this since— Her senses had never been shocked like this.

Out of sheer automatic self-preservation she fought him, but it was like a puppy yapping at the heels of a lumbering bear: The ammunition was hardly adequate for the battle.

The layers of muscle padding his shoulders easily absorbed the blows of her small fists, and she couldn't seem to get the necessary leverage to kick him. And struggling out of his grasp was impossible, given his enormous strength.

In any case, the battle lasted all of five seconds. Teddy felt her own strength draining away, as if he'd managed to uncork a dam inside her, and she became vividly conscious of her body's response to his. There was an instant of shocked immobility, and then a passion she'd never known before rose in a tidal wave. Her mouth opened almost wildly to the fierce insistence of his, and the possessive thrust of his tongue sent a curl of fire licking at her senses.

Teddy promptly forgot everything else. Her arms curved around his neck, her fingers delighting in the thick silk of his hair. His arms were around her, one hand curving around the swell of her bottom to hold her against him and the other across her back so that his fingers lay beneath her arm, touching her breast.

She was hardly aware that the outer curve of her other breast was pressed against the gun he wore.

The searing demand of his mouth branded her, and she could feel the most deeply buried responses her body could claim rising to meet him, to give what he demanded of her. Her breasts throbbed and ached intolerably, and when she felt the swelling response of his body, her own quivered with readiness. For the first time in her life a hollow need whispered yearningly that her female body had been designed for this, intended, fated for this, and that instinct was a seduction she couldn't fight.

It was insane, of course, wild, mad, inescapably crazy. It was something that didn't *happen*. Not like this, not so quickly and violently. Not with a stranger—and a dangerous one, at that. But Teddy could no more fight the turbulent awakening of her body than she could move mountains or halt an earthquake. It was a force of nature, one never intended to be understood or mastered by so frail a thing as a human.

The realization flitted briefly though Teddy's mind, and she accepted it. Her body knew more certainly than her intellect that this was *right*.

She held back nothing. Her small, slender body moved sensuously against his hard frame, and her mouth fed his hunger while demanding with her own. She wanted him.

Zach had acted on impulse, kissing her because it would quiet her and because he wanted to kiss her, had wanted to since the middle of the night while he sat and watched her sleep. But he had not been prepared for this. This explosion. This detonation of something raw and devastating.

If it had been only his own response, he might have been able to fight it, but her fiery reaction was more than even his great strength and control could master. Though generally holding himself aloof, he was a physical, sensual man and not in the habit of denying himself. And with this slender, feminine woman moving seductively against him, he wasn't prepared to start now.

Teddy wasn't aware of movement but automatically identified the softness of the cot when she was lowered onto it. A dull thud told her he had managed to get out of his shoulder harness and had dropped the gun to the floor. She felt bereft when his mouth left hers, but instant pleasure replaced the loss as his lips trailed down her neck. She could feel the heavy weight of his leg thrown across hers, and her fingers delightedly explored the corded power of his muscled back.

He was raised on an elbow, one hand beneath her neck and the other parting the buttons of her flannel shirt and tugging it from the waistband of her jeans.

Teddy had wondered how she would respond in sexual passion—or even if she *would*. Since she had never felt more than a mild tingle, she had begun to wonder if that was in the cards at all for her. But she had thought about it, as women do, wondered if she would be awkward or self-conscious. Wondered if she would be passive or passionate, mindless or detached and analytical. It had always been the latter during the kisses and fumbling caresses of the past.

Now she knew. She hadn't imagined herself frantically coping with stubborn buttons, hadn't dreamed that the sounds of an overpowering need could tear loose from her throat as if they were alive and on the wing.

She felt his hand deal with the final button and sweep the flannel aside, and her eyes opened, dazed, to fix themselves on his taut face. Out of habit she had worn no bra, and Zach caught his breath when her small, full breasts were bared to his hungry gaze. His hand slid slowly up over her quivering middle until it closed gently, fiercely, on one creamy mound, and Teddy gasped at the instant, searing pleasure of that touch.

Her eyes closed briefly as a surge of hot weakness flowed through her, and a moan followed the gasp when he drew a tightening coral nipple into his mouth. Wildly, she pushed his unbuttoned shirt off his shoulders, and as he yanked the garment off and tossed it aside, she was exploring the powerful, hair-roughened expanse of his chest with fascinated hands.

She wanted to touch him, had to touch him, but the sensations rocketing through her body sparked a total absorption in what his touch was doing to her. She could only hold on to him, her nails digging into his shoulders, while wave after wave of pleasure assaulted her.

Her body had a mind of its own. The hungry pull of his mouth seemed to be drawing something out of her and replacing it with fire, and she moved restlessly, impatient. The deep muscles of her belly contracted strongly when his hand slid caressingly downward, and she didn't realize he had unfastened her jeans until his hand slid beneath them to toy with the elastic edge of her panties.

She felt as well as heard him speak, the vibration of his words a new pleasure against her breast.

"This isn't the time or place," he murmured huskily, "but I want you, Teddy. Right now . . . I have to have you."

She bit her lip and forced a heartfelt agreement out of her tight throat. "Yes. Yes, Zach . . ."

His lips were still at her breast, stringing hot kisses and tiny stinging bites that were driving her mad, and his voice was deeper, more hoarse, when he spoke again.

"I didn't come up here prepared for this. I can't protect you."

Teddy didn't much care, but the question in his voice was clear, and she answered it honestly, warmed by his concern and concentrating on just getting the words out. "I've never had a reason to worry about that. But it's all right, I think—it's the wrong time."

If she'd had the breath, she would have confided that the women in her family had difficulty in conceiving, anyway, and that her doctor had warned her she would probably have the same difficulty. But she didn't have the breath or the patience to explain about that.

"Zach . . ." Something was wrong, she realized. He was lifting his head, staring down at her with something wild in his eyes.

"What are you saying?" he asked tightly.

She looked at him, a chill of bewilderment cooling her passion. "I—that it's all right."

"You said you'd never had to worry about it before. Why?" he bit out.

Teddy could feel the hard tension in the nape of his neck, tension her fingers instinctively tried—and failed—to ease. "I never had a reason to," she confessed finally, her voice small and husky.

"You're a virgin?" he demanded bluntly.

"Does it matter?" It was an answer.

Zach abruptly pulled away and jerked into a sitting position, his broad back turned to her. "Hell, yes, it matters!" he snapped violently. "I want you, Teddy, but I'll be damned if I'll be the first man you take to your bed!"

"Actually, it's your bed," she murmured, drawing her shirt closed with trembling fingers and hastily fastening her jeans before she sat up.

He threw one searing look over his shoulder at her, a scornful refusal to respond to that.

Teddy was coping fiercely with the coldness of rejection, even as she tried to understand what had caused it. Her pride was spared the possibility that it was lack of desire on his part, so it was either her virginity or their lack of protection. And since it was something she could explain away, Teddy chose the latter, even though she had a hollow feeling that wasn't it.

"I wouldn't get pregnant, Zach. The women in my family have been lucky to produce even one child each generation, going back over a hundred years. It's . . . it's a chemical thing or . . . or something."

He said nothing.

She buttoned her shirt slowly, staring at his broad, tense back. Oddly enough, she didn't feel self-conscious, and there was no regret at all for what had almost happened. Only that it hadn't. Her body still ached for him. And Teddy, though Zach couldn't know it—yet—was a very tenacious lady. So she concentrated on getting to the bottom of this.

"Afraid I'd yell rape to the police?" she asked lightly.

"No."

"Well, that's something, anyway. What, then, Zach? Afraid I'd hang around your neck forever because you'd be my first lover? Is that it?"

Zach refused to look at her. He was holding on to control with every muscle and gritted teeth, and only his certain knowledge of the dangers inherent in their situation allowed him that fragile command. His body pulsed heavily and his heart was still pounding against his ribs, but his mind was cold and clear.

He wouldn't go through it again. He *wouldn't*.

"Zach?"

But if that wasn't it, he thought, then maybe . . . "Why me?" he asked harshly. "Just tell me."

She hesitated, licking her dry lips, sensing her answer to his question was terribly important. And she didn't know the answer he needed to hear. "Because . . . I want you. Because I've never felt that way before. Because I—oh, dammit, Zach, what d'you want me to say?"

They had known each other less that twelve hours. Zach knew he had been right.

"You've said it." He reached down for his shirt, then rose quickly and shrugged into it, striding toward the door. "If I catch you outside this cabin," he said, "I'll turn you over my knee."

Angry and bewildered, she snapped, "If I were into that sort of thing, I'd take you up on it!"

He turned at the door, his face hard and remote, a glitter of promise in his eyes. "Don't push me, Teddy," he warned. "You wouldn't like the results. I meant what I said about shipping your little butt out of here."

Sweetly, she said, "My *pretty* little butt, remember?"

For a moment, just an instant, she thought that would get a laugh out of him. But then he was gone.

Teddy leaned back against the wall and hugged her raised knees, frowning. She didn't think much about her motives, partly because things looked confused in that direction and partly because she knew understanding wouldn't change anything.

Firstly, it didn't matter that she knew next to nothing about him or about what he was doing here. She had always relied on her instincts—they had never yet failed her—and her instincts told her now that Zach was a man she could trust.

Secondly, Teddy was damned if she'd allow the first man who had ignited her senses to reject her.

She let the question of motive stop right there.

What remained, logically, was the question of what she could do about the problem. Obviously, she first had to find out why Zach was so rabid on the subject of virgins. And she'd have to walk a fine line to keep from interfering with whatever he was doing here so that he wouldn't send her away.

So. She had a few days, possibly a week or more, in which to convince a tremendously strong, taciturn man of stubborn disposition, uncertain temper, and powerful desires—who might or might not be doing something on the shady side of legal—that her virtuous state held no dangers at all for him.

And to aid her cause were the simple facts that he was more or less stuck here, more or less stuck with her, had already admitted in word and deed that he wanted her, and was obviously a highly sexed man who was unaccustomed to living a celibate life.

Teddy caught herself giggling, and she wondered what her mother would have said if she'd been aware of her daughter's methodical summation of the problem.

"Go for it, Teddy."

Yes, she decided, that's what her mother would have said. Their names had changed through marriage over the generations, but Teddy could indeed trace her bloodline back through a long line of women who had been thrifty in almost every way. They tended to love only one man whom they always married—she had no idea about lovers—produce one child, invariably a girl; live in one house from marriage until burial; possess at least one slightly unusual trait or talent—Teddy's was an instinctive communication with animals—use their hormones for things other than growing tall—not one had been taller than five-foot-three; were red-haired, left-handed, myopic, resistant to most illnesses; and always stronger than they looked. Her mother had broken this pattern in only one respect: With great effort she had managed to produce a second daughter.

The genes handed down all these years from a long-ago and highly improbable mating of a highland Scot and a fiery-eyed Gypsy girl had remained dominant regardless of the fact that two Englishmen, a Spaniard, an Italian, two Cherokee Indians, a cowboy from Montana, an industrialist from California, a politician from New Hampshire, and half a dozen other hopefuls had all thrown their very best into the genetic pool.

Teddy's father—the industrialist from California—had insisted that he'd tried his best but hadn't managed to bequeath to his daughters his height, his excellent vision, his right-handedness, or his inborn ability to make a decent pot of coffee. And since Teddy was their first offspring, gleefully produced after ten years of trying, and since logically, her parents had expected her to be their solitary one, her father, in a rare burst of loquaciousness, had bequeathed to her instead a grand name which by rights should have been divided between at least three girls. (Jennifer was Jennifer Leigh, so it seemed her father had gotten it partially out of his system with Teddy and was too shocked by Jenny's surprising and successful arrival to be creative.)

At any rate, Teddy had a solid line of slightly offbeat, definitely determined, prudent ladies at her back, and she had no intention of shaming them by meekly accepting rejection.

Zach Steele didn't have a chance.

She smiled to herself, then suddenly exclaimed as a memory prodded her. She leaned forward to look down at the floor. It was there as she'd thought, looking deceptively innocent and unthreatening in its holster.

What had he said? He'd forgotten he wore a gun because he'd become used to it? A man like Zach, she thought, would be aware that his gun was not in its accustomed place. He'd feel the lack of it automatically.

But Zach had been upset when he'd left, she realized. Upset enough to walk out of the cabin and leave his gun lying on the floor. And that told her two things. He did indeed trust her enough to leave her, awake and aware, in the cabin with weapons another "hostage" would have turned on him. And he had had to fight himself—as well as her—to reject her.

Teddy leaned back against the wall, smiling.

It was a start.

Three

When Zach returned to the cabin, the appetizing scents of bacon and pancakes filled the small room, coffee was bubbling on the stove, and Teddy was whistling cheerfully as she set the small table with paper plates and plastic utensils. He closed the door behind him and just stood there for a moment, watching her. She had put her hair up in a ponytail, which made her look ridiculously sweet and innocent, and about sixteen. Zach had automatically checked the dates on her driver's license and knew she was ten years older.

He glanced toward the bed, seeing that she had hung his shoulder harness over one of the posts and getting the point of that: She hadn't forgotten it, she knew it was there, and she had no intention of using the gun.

Zach couldn't figure her out. Other than during the first hour or so of her captivity, she hadn't reacted in any expectable way to the situation, and

God knew she looked calm enough for a woman who had so nearly taken her first lover half an hour ago.

As for himself, Zach was more than a little grim. The icy water of the stream had done little to cool his desire, and even with a mind hell-bent on avoiding sex, he knew just how precarious his control with her really was.

He wanted her. In fact, he couldn't recall a time when he'd wanted a woman more. Her soft, delightfully feminine body had fit into his arms with utter perfection, and the fire caged in that slim, delicate form had ignited his senses in a way he'd never known before. He didn't doubt she was a virgin, and yet her innate capacity for passion was staggering and intriguing, tantalizing his mind with its promise.

She looked across the room at him just then, and Zach knew without a shadow of doubt that she had read his mind. He could literally feel something inside him turn over with a thud but had no idea what it was, or what it meant.

"Breakfast is ready." Her voice was light and casual. "You'd better taste the coffee with care, though."

Welcoming the distraction, Zach moved to the table and lifted the cup she indicated. The first sip of hot liquid nearly choked him, and he looked at her in disbelief. "I thought I'd tasted the worst coffee ever made, but this—! What the hell *is* this?"

Unoffended, Teddy sat down at the table and shrugged. "My father says that making good coffee is an inborn talent. Unfortunately, it isn't one of mine. Sorry." She began buttering the sack of pancakes on her plate, adding, "You really did come prepared to stay a while, didn't you? Even butter and syrup. Who made out the shopping list "

"I did." He carried his cup to the sink, calmly emptied it, dumped the rest, then made a fresh pot. When it was ready, he carried his refilled cup back to the table and lifted a questioning brow at her.

"I'm used to it," she said, indicating the remains of her own coffee.

"You must have a cast-iron stomach," he commented, sitting down.

"Probably. I'm a good cook aside from coffee, however, so you don't have to worry about food poisoning."

She had made enough to feed an army, and after the first tentative taste confirmed her promise, Zach, in silent appreciation, cleared away most of what she'd prepared. Teddy waited until he had nearly finished before she quietly dropped her bomb.

"What was her name?"

After an instant's hesitation he grunted, "Who?" and sat back, sipping his coffee.

Teddy met his stony gaze squarely, her own eyes calm and reflective. "That woman whose first lover you became. The one who somehow burned you. Did she get too demanding, Zach, was that it?"

"Drop it, Teddy."

She smiled just a little and softly quoted: " 'He went back through the Wet Wild Woods, waving his wild tail and walking by his wild lone. But he never told anybody.' Kipling. You don't tell anybody, either, do you, Zach? You just go your own way, alone and dangerous and stoic. Have you ever let a woman get close to you? Have you ever let down your guard that much?"

"Once." He hadn't meant to say it, and the bleak sound of his own voice startled him. And then he saw that her eyes had softened, gone impossibly tender, and even though he *knew* it wasn't real, he couldn't look away from her small, vital face.

"I'm sorry she hurt you."

He found himself responding without thought, lost in the satiny brown depths of her eyes. "It wasn't her fault."

"What happened, Zach?" she asked gently. She almost held her breath, painfully aware of just how important it was that he tell her about this.

"It . . . happened, that's all. It just happened."

"Tell me." She had unconsciously lowered her voice almost to a croon, instinctively using the tone that almost magically caused animals to trust her. Even wild ones. And she never thought—then—that it was the jungle-born part of Zach that was responding, that it was there he caged the hurts of his life.

Still without thought, he told her.

"I had set up a security system for an American businessman in South America. His family was there, and he worried about their safety. Rightly, as it turned out. His daughter was kidnapped. They'd breached my security system, and I felt responsible. So I went after her."

Teddy felt her eyes widen at his flat tone, the utter simplicity of his words. What he had done was matter-of-fact and reasonable to him, as if every man was sometimes called upon to wade into shark-infested waters to retrieve something the swirling currents had carried away from him.

"They had taken her deep into the jungle, but I managed to get to her. And get her safely away from them. But they were after us, and we had miles of jungle to cross before we reached safety. It was hellish and dangerous, and the conditions were primitive in a way she'd never experienced before. She had no one to turn to but me. So she did."

Zach's mouth twisted, but he never looked away from Teddy's eyes. "I found out too late she'd never had a lover. Still, it didn't seem to matter. She said she'd never been in love before, either. And even though I knew the jungle was no place for love, I believed her. I believed her."

Because I felt it too.

He didn't have to say it, but Teddy heard it. She drew a deep breath. "What happened?"

His smile was bleak and rather frightening. "We got back to civilization. And with the mists of the jungle gone, I didn't fit her image of what her husband should be. I was hard, she said. I frightened her. So I left." And his next words seemed wrenched from him with a raw, torn sound. "I found out later— she had an abortion."

Teddy stared into the diamond-bright sheen of his gray eyes and felt a throb of pain for him. No wonder, she thought dimly, he was rabid about being a woman's first lover and distrustful of "the wrong time" for conception.

"I understood," he said, calmer, his voice going remote. "What happened between us was an accident, a mistake. She didn't want to pay for that mistake, and it was her right to make the decision."

"What if she had told you?" Teddy hadn't realized she was going to ask him and almost held her breath for his answer.

For the first time Zach looked away from her. His eyes were blind, opaque. He shoved his chair back and rose to his feet, his lean face expressionless. "I love kids," he said abruptly, and turned away to go over to the clutter of equipment on the makeshift shelf.

Teddy sat where she was, staring at his back. She was unaware of the hot tears brimming over her eyes and searing their way down her cheeks. She was aware of nothing but what her heart was crying out to him.

How long has it been, Zach? How long have you tortured yourself? How many times have you asked yourself what you would have done if she'd told you about your child? Do you wonder if you would have had the right to ask that she give birth to your baby? Do you wonder if you would have asked, rightfully or not?

She got up slowly, stiffly, and began clearing the table. Zach was sitting at his equipment, earphones in place and closing her out, signaling flatly his refusal to talk anymore. And Teddy respected his wishes, partly because he had withdrawn so completely and partly because he had told her what she guessed he had told no one else. Or at least no other woman.

It was enough. For now it was enough.

She occupied herself in quiet, hearing the occasional clicking of three different tape recorders that seemed to go on and shut off in response to some silent signal. She dug out her deck of playing cards and sat on the bed, playing solitaire and thinking.

He had told her, and in telling her, he had triggered something deep inside her. What was it? she wondered. There had been something deep in his eyes. . . .

And then she remembered. Years before, she had helped to track a cougar that had escaped a small circus and disappeared into the hills. She had found him, and her tearful, bitter swearing had brought the others to see what she had found. The cougar, young and powerful, had two legs caught and mangled by the cruel steel traps that some fool had set, and he'd had to be destroyed.

But during her few moments alone with the big cat, Teddy had looked into the eyes that held such terrible pain and yet were stoic, proud. Those proud, anguished eyes had seemed to say, "It was my own stupid fault"; he hadn't blamed the cruel human who'd set the trap. The eyes of an intelligent creature with a wild heart, a creature that would have dragged his mangled body away and licked his wounds alone, given a choice.

Alone . . .

Teddy felt a wave of dizziness pass over her suddenly, and she seemed to be somewhere else. Behind her closed eyes, images flashed like a film reel gone mad, then slowed and steadied, and the focus sharpened.

A young soldier, his fatigues drenched and muddied, pushed his way cautiously through a cloying jungle, his gray eyes red-rimmed with weariness but sharp. On his left cheek was a long, thin slash that still trickled blood.

The same man, but older now, worked among a bank of electronic equipment, his long fingers moving with expert precision. But he was still in fatigues.

The street was crowded—it was New York—and the man moved with the silence of a shadow in that concrete jungle, yet his fatigues set him apart from the casual and business dress of the hurrying mass of people all around him.

An office. No, a boardroom. And men with the

hard, tough faces garnered in living in a corporate jungle. A dark and handsome man sat at the head of the table, and his rather cold blue eyes warmed when he looked back at the man in fatigues standing to indicate a set of blueprints on display.

Another place, screaming of danger. Men with guns, and a dark-haired woman and two teenage girls with terrified faces. A swift, hard battle, with the man in fatigues taking down a gunman in effortless silence.

A storm-tossed island and a flimsy vessel. A blond man and a man with copper hair and a woman with a beautiful face and sea-green eyes. And the man in fatigues carrying guns and explosives, and another man brought out of a cell. And a large vessel that became an even larger one, and champagne to celebrate—

A rotund little man with brilliant eyes in a cherub's face, a man with a voice of authority who thought he was Charlemagne and Richard and Lincoln and Machiavelli. . . . And the man in fatigues gathering equipment and going to war again, because it was wrong not to, and this time he would fight alone.

The images whirled madly, confused, as if some capricious winds snatched at them. And then they steadied, focused, and she saw him again, And he was no longer set apart by the clothing of a warrior. He was no longer alone.

Teddy opened her eyes, the images gone as swiftly as they had come. She was sitting up, hugging her knees, the cards forgotten. She was shocked, as anyone would be when confronted by the inexplicable, but she was not frightened. She had, in a sense, been preparing for that dizzying journey all her life.

It happened only once, her mother had told her. And who knew if it came from a Scot with second sight or a Gypsy with an enigmatic gift. But it came once in a lifetime. An intense vision of past and present and future. A gift of understanding when that was most needed.

And Teddy looked at Zach, seeing that her silent journey had not disturbed him. She looked at him—and understood.

He had worn no uniform in the streets of New York. No uniform in boardrooms or in small houses where dangerous things happened. He had worn no uniform on a storm-battered island. Those parts of the images had been symbolic.

He was a warrior, a man of hard danger, born in the hazardous jungles of the world. A lone wolf who had friends but who stood apart from them by choice. *"He walked by himself, and all places were alike to him."* Kipling again. Wise Kipling.

She knew now why her memory of the cougar had risen in her mind. Because Zach was like that big cat. He didn't blame the woman who had hurt him so badly. He blamed himself. It was his own stupid fault for getting into that mess. And now he'd be damned if he did it again. He wouldn't let himself step into the jaws of a trap and watch it mangle a part of him.

Teddy drew a ragged breath, even her determined nature staggered by the odds against her. She guarded the small nugget of hope nestling inside her, the promise of the final image that had flashed before her, but she also knew how tough the battle would be.

She had to tame the wild heart of a jungle warrior, had to chip away at the suspicious, protective layers of iron he had wrapped himself in. She had to coax a lone wolf to walk willingly at her side.

She knew what her motive was now.

And she knew he'd never believe her.

"I have to go out for a while," he told her.

Teddy was still sitting as before, but her forehead was resting against her raised knees. She didn't dare look at him, struggling to master a tumult of emotions every bit as primitive as the physical sensations of the morning had been. Her understanding of him and of what he was to her had somehow severed the threads of her control, leaving her nakedly vulnerable.

"All right," she responded.

"You won't—?"

"I won't try to leave." She felt more than heard him step closer, and grappled against the urge to look at him.

"Are you all right, Teddy?" The stiffness was leaving his voice, replaced by concern.

She hugged her knees harder. "Yes." *How insane! I've never been less right in my life! Or more right. Oh, God, help me.* She could feel his hesitation, the instant's suspension. Then he was shrugging into his shoulder harness and gathering a few other things. She kept her eyes closed, but she could almost see what he was doing. The door closed quietly.

Teddy looked up—and froze. "That's cheating," she whispered.

He was standing at the door, staring at her. He had known she wouldn't look up until she thought him gone, she realized. And now he was gazing at her, his brows drawing together in a frown, and she knew her face was white, her eyes wild.

Well, dammit, she thought half hysterically, a woman didn't fall in love with a lone-wolf warrior every day. It was bound to be a shock to her system.

"Something is wrong," he said, taking a step toward her.

She was quite literally gritting her teeth, fighting a powerful, wild, mad urge to grab him with both hands and hold on for dear life. Somewhere in her was a small astonishment that she could feel with such devastating strength, but another part of her was gloriously elated by it. It would require, she thought, a strength like that to catch and hold a wolf.

"Teddy?"

She felt herself smiling, and wondered what kind of smile it looked like. It felt dreadful. In a wonderfully conversational tone with only a trace of huskiness, she said, "If I were you, I'd leave. You see, I'm not quite safe at the moment."

He looked bewildered—as well he might, she thought.

She drew a deep breath and held on to her knees tightly. "Zach, I don't want to make you mad just now, and if I told you what I'm feeling, I'm afraid you'd get mad. You'll get mad, anyway, of course, but I can't handle it at the moment."

"Dammit, Teddy—"

As the lesser of two evils, she told him part of what she was feeling. "I want you," she said baldly. "Rather badly. So would you go away for a while, please?"

A hot flare of response lit his eyes almost instantly,

but then he swore softly and quickly turned away. And this time he really did leave the cabin.

Teddy just sat there trembling for a long time, trying to find some way of controlling these incredible feelings. She was finally able to get up and went into the bathroom on shaking legs to splash cold water on her face. It didn't really help. She hadn't really expected it to.

Good Lord, she thought bemusedly, how could a body that didn't fully know what it was all about *want* it so badly? And what about these other feelings, the tangle of love and tenderness and pain and longing? How did people *survive* this? She was aching, trembling, hot inside with a need that seemed to be tearing her apart.

She wanted Zach. It sounded so simple, but everything she felt told her it wasn't. She wanted to sob, to laugh, to cry out wildly in order to release whatever was tearing at her to get out. She wanted to hold on tightly to Zach because he would anchor her in the chaos of a world gone mad.

If a bargain with the devil would have assured her of his love, she would have fought her way to hell and demanded it.

Teddy paced. She walked the confined space of the cabin, jerkily at first, then methodically, groping for control, for exhaustion, for anything that would ease the torment. She ate three apples and half a bunch of bananas, instinctively trying to assuage an aching hunger that no amount of food would satisfy.

And finally it was exhaustion that she found. She curled up on the bed, hugging a pillow that was too soft and not nearly large enough, her eyes stinging hotly and her body throbbing with the dull soreness of something battered. Her world had narrowed to this, and no one had warned her that it hurt so much.

It was stillness that woke her. Stillness inside of her. The emotions that had scratched and clawed to escape were quiet now, waiting for . . . something. She could still feel them, but what had battered before stroked gently now. As if a storm had passed, leaving quiet and peace in its wake.

No, she thought, not quite peace. She was just in the eye of the hurricane, that was all.

She sat up slowly, pushing the pillow away, realizing that she had held it so fiercely in sleep that her arms and shoulders ached. She stretched stiffly, feeling tired, looking at Zach where he sat at the table and watched her silently.

She glanced at the equipment, murmuring, "You aren't listening anymore."

"The tapes are voice-activated," he said. "I won't miss anything." And then he frowned, staring at her curiously pale face and wondering what it was about her casual questions that pulled things from him with such effortless ease. It was a fleeting concern, however; he was worried about her.

Teddy misread the frown. "Oh, I don't care what you're doing up here, Zach," she said wearily. "I probably know, anyway. Not why, maybe, but certainly what. There's a house through the woods, near where my car died, and you've got it bugged. I heard an engine in the distance just before you went out. You knew they were gone and you went out there to check on something. Okay? If somebody pulls out my fingernails, that's all I could tell them."

"It's serious, Teddy," he said, a little harsh. "And damned dangerous."

"Right," she murmured, pulling the rubber band from her hair to free the ponytail. "Stolen gems and art treasures, I'd guess. I don't know why they'd be way up here. Because it's unlikely, I suppose. Because that house out there is a conduit, maybe, passing the stuff through to somewhere else."

Zach gazed at her for a long moment, bothered by this new, vulnerable mood of hers. Bothered by the way she had slept, hugging the pillow with a kind of desperation. And he was also disturbed because she didn't seem to grasp the danger of this, and that could get her killed. He didn't like what he felt at the thought of her being in real danger.

"You've got part of it," he admitted suddenly. "Gems and artwork stolen recently are finding their way to that house. But if that were the only thing, the police could move in now."

"And you suspect there's a good deal more to it." She leaned back against the wall, watching him and very aware of the dull ache of need inside her. The storm . . .

"Yes. The valuables in the house have been carefully acquired and are intended to be used in barter."

"For what?"

"Guns."

Teddy frowned. "You mean that the people in the house gather up a bunch of priceless art and jewelry and then trade them to somebody for weapons?"

"That's what I mean."

"But why? How?"

"Those are the questions I'm up here to answer. The best guess for 'why' is that they're going to turn around and sell the guns to needy armies in Third World countries—or terrorists. Or maybe that's what they are themselves. We don't have any guess at all for 'how,' but since it's not all that easy to get large shipments of weapons out of this country, it's a safe bet that somebody official is being well paid to turn a blind eye."

She stared at him wonderingly. "But who would be able to get a shipment that big into the country in the first place?"

Zach wondered fleetingly how long it had been since he himself might have asked that innocent question. Years. A lifetime. He sighed a little. "Anybody with enough money and the right connections. In this case, we think there are two men, both very wealthy and as pure as the driven snow. Each is a collector of rare artwork and gems, with private vaults built expressly for everything not acquired legitimately. They covet art and don't give a sweet damn how they get it."

After a moment she said slowly, "So you're up here to trace the—route? Where the artwork goes from here, who gets it, and how the guns get out of the country?"

"That's it, roughly. The valuables are stolen by a well-organized ring of thieves; Interpol has them pegged but is waiting for us to get this end of the mess nailed down. A professional courtesy. We know how the stuff gets this far. Another—someone else is working on the matter of how so many arms are being sold to private citizens."

"Another agent," she murmured.

Zach hesitated, then said firmly, "I'm temporary. Paying back a favor, you might say."

"I see. No badge."

"Not officially, no."

Teddy nodded. "So, you're going to follow the art-work when it's shipped out?"

"That's the plan. I've had the place bugged hoping to hear something interesting about how the trade will be made, but so far there's been nothing. They're waiting for a few more things to arrive before the stuff is moved."

"Do you know where the shipment of arms is?"

"We know. And somebody will be watching care-fully to see how it's taken out of the country. Need-less to say, the guns will never reach their destination."

After a moment he said, "Sheer luck that we found a trail to follow. People who steal artwork don't usu-ally involve themselves with arms—and vice versa. But we know this is one organization: The thieves and the men who trade the valuables for arms. We also know they've completed trades successfully in the past."

Teddy looked at him, conscious of the stillness that remained. It encased her, as protective as a blanket of peace. But she could feel the storm. Wait-ing. Swirling all around her. The threat of it was the promise of that terrible need. That aching anguish that she could feel now only dully.

"Why tell me this now?" she asked finally, quietly.

His mouth firmed, and a muscle tightened in his jaw. "I said we knew they'd been successful before. They've also killed. Coldly and with utter business-like professionalism. They don't leave loose ends dan-gling, Teddy. They're killers, pure and simple. I wanted you to know that, to believe that. Every hour they remain in the house increases the chance that somebody'll find one of the bugs. And if they do, they'll start looking. For us."

She thought about that. They were close enough, she knew, to be easily found. She wasn't frightened by that, though, because Zach was here; with danger threatening, he was an immensely comforting man, and she knew without even thinking about it that he would take care of her, protect her.

Oddly enough, her only reaction to Zach's disclosure of his lawful, if unofficial, reason for being here was a mental *Well, of course.* Some inner part of her had never believed he was here for a nefarious purpose.

Teddy listened to the distant thunder of her inner storm and wondered how long she could hold it at bay. Not long. Not long at all. And her mind methodically considered the sequence of events that measured the time left to her.

"I see. So when the artwork is shipped out, you'll follow?"

"Yes."

"I thought you didn't have a car up here."

"I don't. I have a Jeep."

She considered berating him for splitting hairs earlier but dismissed it as unimportant. "Oh. And you'll drop me off somewhere along the way?"

His mouth firmed again. "I'll put you on a plane to your sister. And I'll see to it that there's a replacement for your car waiting for you."

Teddy looked at him, feeling tired, feeling too many other things. "Remember the Alamo," she murmured.

"What?"

She was really too tired to fight him, to fight his mistaken belief—and it had to be that—that she was being overwhelmed by the unusual circumstances surrounding them. That she was being seduced by those circumstances, rather than by him. Too tired. But she didn't have a choice.

"I'm a sucker for lost causes," she said, clarifying nothing except to herself.

"Teddy, what are you talking about?" he asked with vast patience.

She held the storm at bay. "Some women are stupid," she said. "That doesn't mean we all are. Some women can be deceived by their own emotions—that doesn't mean we all can be."

He knew what she was talking about now, and his face closed down into remoteness. In a flat, decisive tone he said, "You haven't been listening to me. This is a dangerous situation, and you will be out of it just as soon as possible."

And out of my life.

Teddy rolled the dice and watched to see how they landed. "I love you, Zach."

His head moved faintly, an uncontrolled and unconscious gesture of negation. "No. This time yesterday you didn't even know me."

She laughed softly, almost without being aware of it. "Yes. But things always happen fast in my life. I should have expected love to be no different."

"You don't know anything about me," he told her flatly.

It would not be a good time to prove that she did indeed know a great deal about him; it would be too difficult to explain just now. Instead, she shrugged. "That doesn't seem to matter."

"It should matter. It would—if we were somewhere else."

Teddy shook her head. "No, I don't think so. I know what I feel."

His eyes narrowed, and his entire body looked taut. In a voice that was harsh he said, "Then know you'll get over it. Know it won't last the time it'll take to get down off this mountain. Know that, Teddy."

It was my own stupid fault, and I won't let it happen again.

She fought a rising despair, wondering how she could convince him. And then she knew that only time would convince him—if she were granted that time and the ability to use it—and the storm pushed inward to remind her of the anguish of uncertainty and waiting. She could literally feel herself pale, and she saw his hard eyes flicker.

"What if I don't get over it?" she asked.

"You will." He swore suddenly, harshly. "Don't look at me like that!"

Teddy dropped her gaze to focus on her knees. Instinct told her that no amount of arguing with Zach would help. Not here, at least, and not now. And the only avenue left open to her was the disturbing, painful one leading to the storm she felt . . . and which he felt at least partially. She wanted him; he wanted her. That was all she had.

"All right," she said softly. "Let's assume for the sake of argument that I'll get over it. Maybe you're right and I will." Every word was a stab, but she bore the pain. "Still, neither of us can deny that we want each other. And there's no risk of pregnancy."

"There's always a risk," he said, interrupting curtly.

She looked at him then, and in her eyes was the pain of someone who loved children and knew only too well that she would be lucky indeed to have even one of her own. "No risk," she repeated softly. "It took my parents ten years to get me, and Jenny was nothing less than a miracle—the doctor said so. Jenny's miscarried twice, and my doctor tells me I'll be lucky if I get even that far."

She squared her shoulders and met his unreadable eyes with a bedrock certainty in her own. "Everyone has their own beliefs and their own right to them, and I would never judge them by my own standards. But there is one thing you have to know, Zach, one thing you can be certain of. If, by some incredible bit of luck, I managed to conceive, there wouldn't be an abortion. That's something I could never do."

He looked away first, jerkily, something hot and a little wild flickering suddenly in his eyes. "All the more reason," he said roughly.

She drew a deep, shuddering breath. "Then you won't make love to me?"

"No." It was a bitten-out sound.

Teddy felt the surge of the storm and chewed her lip briefly. No pride. Dammit, it even stole pride. But that was only a fleeting realization, a distant pain.

She had rolled the dice and lost. But she wasn't finished. She would gamble everything she had, keep rolling the dice until there was nothing left.

She looked at her watch, struggling to bring it into focus and absently realizing that she'd slept for several hours. "Those men are still gone?"

For a moment Zach seemed startled, as if he'd braced himself for argument, for persuasion. "Yes," he said finally, sending her an oblique glance.

Teddy slid off the cot, straightening her clothes with automatic movements. She was aware of his eyes following her, and strove to keep her face calm.

But behind the facade she was thinking with a clarity born of need.

He wouldn't believe her, wouldn't *let* himself believe her. All right, then. So be it. If she couldn't convince his stubborn mind, she'd work on other parts of him. Somehow. The big, tough body that she knew wanted hers. And the heart she was sure lay hidden deep within him, encased in the protective metallic armor of a warrior.

She wondered if the Gypsy had fought for her Scot and thought that she probably had.

Teddy wished she had seen just a bit more of that final image, wished she could be *sure*. But how often was certainty of the future given to mortals?

Silent and at least outwardly calm, she began preparing an evening meal for them.

Four

Sarah Lewis was a familiar sight in the building housing Long Enterprises, and she knew her way around quite well. Greetings followed her as she made her way up to the fifteenth floor, where she expected to find her husband despite the fact that his own suite of offices was two floors up. She hardly needed an identification badge to gain access to the security-conscious fifteenth, but she wore one never-theless—and the security guard at the desk near the elevator didn't even glance at it.

"Morning, Mrs. Lewis."

"Hi, Phil." Her voice was soft and a bit shy, and the guard looked with pleasure at her bright hair and serene eyes.

While she signed the register he asked how Junior was doing on this fine morning, and the glow in her eyes seemed to intensify even as she laughed.

"Fine, thanks." She patted her rounded stomach, over which a gay yellow sign imprinted on her terrycloth shirt proclaimed the presence of a baby on board. "Rafferty's here, isn't he?" she asked.

"Yes, ma'am. In Mr. Kendrick's office."

Sarah waved her thanks and went on down the hall. She could hear the steady humming of computers in the offices she passed, but didn't pause until she reached a corner office. The door was open, and she went in, saying as a greeting, "We're going to have to name him Junior; everybody expects it."

"Over my dead body," her husband promised, looking up to smile at her.

"It sounds original to me," Lucas decided without looking up from the computer screen busily flashing data.

"Nobody asked you," Rafferty told him, then lifted a questioning brow at his lovely wife.

"I used a bit of blackmail," she said, sounding not in the least perturbed about it. "Emotional. Looked teary-eyed and anxious. He's treating me like glass these days, so I thought I could probably get away with it. I think pregnant women make him nervous," she added thoughtfully.

Lucas turned from the computer to face them, grinning a little. "Then by all means let's make him nervous."

Rafferty caught his wife's hand and led her to one of the chairs in front of the desk, sitting on the arm of the second one himself. "So what did your esteemed boss cough up?" he asked.

"Not much," she admitted, an expression of frustration briefly crossing her delicate face. "He did confess that Zach *is* working for him, in Colorado of all places. He promised that—this time—he had been completely truthful about the assignment. Zach knows exactly what's going on, according to Hagen,

and is in possession of all relevant information."
She stopped, looking suddenly uneasy.

Lucas sighed and ran a hand through his silvery
hair, while Rafferty cursed quietly.

"All *relevant* information," the investigator repeated
dismally. "Great. If Hagen were directing Grant's
army, his idea of relevant information would be to
tell him to head south."

"I vote we go kill him," Rafferty said in a dispas-
sionate tone.

"Zach will take care of that later," Lucas decided.
"If he lives through this. Hell."

"There has to be some way we can find out what's
going on," Sarah told the men.

Her husband rubbed his jaw thoughtfully, then
looked across the desk at Lucas. "Wonder if Kelsey's
in this one."

"He seems to turn up every time we do," Lucas
agreed.

Correctly reading the men's faces, Sarah objected,
"He'll be low-profile, surely, even if not actually undercover; how will you find him?"

Lucas lifted a brow at Rafferty. "Raven?"

"She could probably find him, even now. And Josh
wasn't at all happy to find out that Zach's 'vacation'
is nothing of the kind. They'll be flying in from
Canada tonight."

Lucas shook his head. "You know, I sometimes
wonder if Hagen really does plan to get all of us into
his little games."

"Don't even think about that," Rafferty begged,
horrified.

After a moment Sarah said, "I can tell you one
thing about Zach's assignment. He surprised Hagen. A coded message came from Zach last night. I

didn't decode it, but it was on Hagen's desk this morning, and he was muttering the last word of the message as if he couldn't believe it."

"What was the message?" Rafferty asked.

Sarah's retentive memory enabled her to recite the message verbatim. "It said: 'Essential you replace with new '66 Impala destroyed in unavoidable circumstances. Have replacement car waiting at Logan Airport, Boston, Friday latest. Held in the name of T. Tyler, noncombatant.' That was it."

Lucas, who had flown up to Boston the day before, winced slightly and said, "I'm glad I didn't know about that when I talked to Jennifer Morton and told her that her sister was fine. Wonder how the car was destroyed? And, even granting that Hagen wouldn't want to replace the car, why would that message surprise him so much?"

They looked at one another uneasily, and Rafferty said, "Hagen kept repeating the word *noncombatant*?"

"Over and over," Sarah confirmed. "As if he simply couldn't believe it."

All of them felt it should mean something, but since they weren't privy to Hagen's thoughts, none of them knew just what that something was.

Zach was proof against most things. Once determined on what was, in fact, a logical and reasonable decision, few had been known to change his mind. Argument rolled off his back like water off a tiled roof, and gentle persuasion failed to penetrate his tough hide and even tougher will. Strong men had been known to pale at the mere thought of attempting to alter his will, and women had exercised their wiles in vain. Even Josh Long, whom Zach respected and loved like a brother, knew better than to try to sway his friend from some personal decision.

So Zach, though grimly aware of his own desire, had little doubt that he could keep things between him and Teddy platonic. But he braced himself for the storm of her persuasion, nonetheless, because he knew women well enough to have accurately read the determination in Teddy's firm little chin.

He braced himself for a storm, mentally blocking the chinks in his willpower and fiercely leashing his own blustering beast. And he settled down to wait it out. But Zach had forgotten that sometimes a gentle rain can seep into places where a gusty downpour would merely batter and roll off in vain.

She said little that second night together, not sulking or brooding, merely thoughtful and silent. She watched him when she thought he didn't see, her great velvety eyes as deep and soft as a doe's. She remained pale, and sometimes she winced, as if something inside her twinged in pain, but to his questions replied only that she was fine. And she said nothing else about wanting or loving him and made no objection when he rolled out a sleeping bag and got into it late that night when the denizens of the house slept.

Nor did she try her hand at seduction. She changed for sleeping but wore a sweatshirt-type nightgown that fell to her knees and fit loosely. And she said good night in a quiet voice when the battery-powered lamp was turned off.

It was some time later that Zach learned there were things more dangerous to chinks than downpours.

There were tears.

He had allowed his own breathing to deepen and

become even but remained awake, staring up at the blackness of the raftered ceiling. He had gotten no sleep the night before and he was tired, but the power of his desire for her tormented him and made sleep impossible. The small room seemed to close in on him, reducing the few feet between his bed and Teddy's until he felt as if he were standing over her and listening to the faint sounds of her breathing.

And they were faint sounds; even in the silence of the cabin, average ears would have heard nothing. But Zach had trained his ears in jungles, and he heard.

He heard the soft, steady breathing, and his mind tortured him with images of her breasts rising and falling. The images taunted him: Creamy mounds that just filled his palms, tipped with coral and heavy with desire. He closed his eyes, fighting himself, remembering why he had to.

Because once, he hadn't. Because once, he had believed eyes looking at him in excited wonder, believed his own tangle of emotions. Desire, as heated and primitive as the jungles it was born in, had deceived him, just as it had deceived her. And deception had not cushioned those final blows. They might not have loved, but the stiffness in her, the fear in her eyes when she looked at him in her father's elegant house, had hurt. And the knowledge that she—

He didn't want to think about that. Didn't want to think about what it had done to him to find that out.

That was why he had to fight himself. Because he couldn't allow anything like that to happen again. What Teddy felt, she believed to be real, and he knew that. But he also knew far better than she could ever know how circumstances and surroundings could deceive the mind, color the emotions.

And he knew he wouldn't be able to bear its happening again. Not with Teddy. Even if there were no consequences of the act, if they became lovers and she afterward looked at him in fear, in the uneasy recognition that he didn't belong in her world, in the real world, he thought it would probably tear him apart.

Odd that he knew that. Odd that he felt so certain—

Zach stiffened suddenly, and something deep inside him lurched with a painful movement. She was crying.

There wasn't a sound to betray her. No sobs or sniffles. Just a break in the even sound of her breathing, a catch that was almost silent. But he knew. As if he were indeed standing over her and watching a silver trail of tears, he knew.

Zach had done many difficult things in his life, from the physically exhausting to the mentally and emotionally draining. But he had never done anything harder than lying there, muscles taut, body aching, listening without moving to the heart-wrenching sounds of Teddy's quiet tears.

She had fallen asleep around an hour later, but it was much longer before Zach followed suit. And he slept heavily, waking with a start just after dawn to find that she was already up and dressed—and he hadn't heard.

How had he not heard, or at least sensed, movements all around him? Did *he* trust to the point of feeling completely unthreatened in her presence? To the point of allowing the ever-vigilant senses born in the jungle to sleep when they had never before slept with someone nearby?

It was a jarring shock to realize that he did trust her that much.

With its windows covered and door tightly fitted, almost no light could find its way into the cabin. Teddy had turned on the battery lamp, and she dropped to one knee beside his sleeping bag before his eyes could no more than begin to open.

Through his lashes he saw only part of her. He saw her hand, braced on her thigh. He saw it lift, reach toward his shoulder, then hesitate, withdraw as a tremor shook the slender fingers. He saw those fingers close over her leg just above the knee and saw the oval nails dig into denim.

"Zach?"

His eyes opened immediately. Unsurprised, she said softly, "One of the tape recorders came on a little while ago. I thought you should know."

He gazed up at her, for a moment forgetting the job he had to do. Only a faintly swollen look around her eyes, a certain tenderness, remained as evidence of tears shed in darkness. Zach clamped his teeth together and nodded, reaching for the zipper of the sleeping bag. "Thanks."

She got up and moved away, toward the stove and the preparations begun for breakfast.

He had slept only in jeans and now shrugged into his shirt as he stood. Leaving it unbuttoned, he went to the equipment shelf, donning the earphones out of habit rather than necessity now that she knew what was going on. The tape had stopped; he rewound it and listened to the conversation that had taken place minutes ago inside the house.

When it was finished, he set up the tape again

and removed the earphones, frowning a little. When he turned, he found her looking at him, a hesitant question in her eyes but not voiced aloud.

"They're expecting the final goods to arrive on Friday morning," he told her. "Then the whole shipment is scheduled to leave for the new owners on Saturday."

Teddy still looked a little quizzical, obviously taking note of his frown. But Zach didn't explain until he stood shaving in the bathroom, glancing out through the open door at her because he couldn't seem to stop looking at her. And even though he wasn't a man given to voicing puzzles aloud, he found that he wanted to talk. He wanted to talk to her.

"It doesn't feel right," he said abruptly.

She paused while setting the table, watching the economical motions of a man who had performed this same task nearly every morning for twenty years. There was something oddly intimate in watching him shave, and Teddy liked it. "What doesn't feel right?" she asked, hoping he would talk to her, confide in her—anything but continue the guarded silence of yesterday.

"Sending the valuables out in a single shipment, which is apparently their plan. I'd expect them to split it up now, to lessen the chances of losing all of it. We're sure there's more than one buyer, probably two, and they don't live in the same city. Not even the same state. If the stuff's going by truck or van, and that seems likely, it'd be more logical to split it up now rather than on the road somewhere."

A part of Teddy's mind listened to and appreciated the points he was making. But another part had gone cold at the first mention of Saturday. If the goods were to be shipped out on Saturday, then so was she. And today was Wednesday.

Fighting off the awful despair, she spoke off the top of her head with no thought. "Maybe the buyers haven't seen the goods yet and plan to meet the truck somewhere to make certain the stuff's authentic before they tell where the guns are waiting. Or has that meeting already taken place?"

Zach was looking at her. "No. No, we think not." He turned his head to gaze into the mirror and cursed softly.

"What?"

He moved to lean against the doorjamb, using a small towel to wipe away the remaining lather. As if to himself, he muttered, "I should have let Josh strangle him last year. It would have saved us all a lot of trouble."

Teddy was bewildered. "Strangle who?"

He sighed. "The federal maestro I've been stupid enough to take orders from," he explained with a certain amount of bitterness.

"I don't understand."

"Let's just say that if I had a brain worthy of the name, I would have learned long ago to distrust the maestro's solemn assurances that he gives his operatives the whole truth and nothing but the truth."

"He kept something from you?" she ventured, still puzzled.

"It's beginning to look that way."

"What? I mean, how do you know?"

Zach didn't answer for a moment, slowly buttoning his shirt as he came into the room. Teddy went ahead and put breakfast on the table, then sat down when he did, and waited. Zach sipped the coffee he had made before going to shave, his expression abstracted.

Teddy started eating and waited until he followed suit before asking again, "What?"

He shrugged. "Nothing I can explain. It should be straightforward from here, everything according to plan. But—it smells. There's something off-center, out of focus. And I don't know what it is."

Teddy couldn't help him really, except to listen. And when she realized that the restlessness in his eyes wasn't due entirely to his worry over elusive things, she could hardly help but be encouraged by it. She'd lain awake for hours the previous night, trying to think of some way of reaching him. And her eyes still ached with her tears of despair.

But if—even now, in the midst of serious concern—he could look at her and want her, then there was still a chance, despite the threat of time running out. Because she was still determined. She loved him, and no matter what Zach thought, that love was very, very real.

He was visibly restless by the time breakfast was finished. The tape recorders had remained inactive, and he rose after a glance at them to help her clear the table. The area near the sink was cramped, and Teddy was all too conscious of his nearness. She could feel the storm hovering, sending warning gusts of wind toward her, and her fragile control began to splinter.

She heard her own voice, calm but husky, speak to him. "Is it dangerous, this off-center thing you're sensing?"

"Everything's dangerous in a situation like this." Zach was standing beside her, her shoulder almost brushing his arm, and he felt oddly winded, as if something were tightening around his chest, squeezing the breath out of him. He tried in vain, to shake off the feeling. "Especially," he added, "something you can't put your finger on."

He reached to put the bread back on the shelf, and before his arm could fall to his side again, he felt her fingers on his forearm below the rolled-up sleeve of his flannel shirt.

"Sometimes," she said, "what you can touch is even more dangerous."

He looked at her hand, creamy pale against the smooth bronze skin of his arm. The hand that was so small and slender and trembled a little. Clearing his throat of some mysterious obstruction, he said, "You should always avoid danger—"

"If you can," she finished. "I can't, Zach."

He looked, finally, at her face. "I can," he told her, the sudden hoarseness of his voice giving the lie to his promise. "I can for both of us."

"You?" She almost laughed, a soft sound that was part humor and part vast understanding. "You were born for danger. Shaped for it." She stepped closer as he automatically turned to face her, and her free hand came to rest on his chest. "You could no more avoid it than another man could willfully stop breathing."

"Teddy—"

"Don't tell me that what I'm feeling is wrong, that it isn't real!" Her eyes held the amber fire of a cat's. "Don't tell me I'll get over it! I don't believe that, Zach, I *won't*!" She drew a deep breath. "But I won't make demands on you, I promise. If—if you don't want to see me when this is over, then I'll understand."

"It'll be you," he muttered, "who won't want to see me."

"Don't count on it." But her voice was half smiling, because he had, with the statement, implied that there would be a time after this. She hoped. Her hands slid up his chest as his found the curve of her hips, and she tried desperately to rein the wild hunger rising in her, half afraid that what was inside her was too abandoned, too violent.

Zach's eyes were half closed, his lashes hiding the darkening gray as he looked broodingly down on her. His hands remained at her hips, and though they held her tautly, it wasn't to draw her closer but to hold her firmly away from him. "No," he said finally, a guttural sound. Before she could react, he stepped away from her abruptly.

"Zach—"

"No, dammit!"

A part of Teddy's emotions took wing then, and she allowed them their fierce, angry flight. "I'm twenty-six years old," she told him furiously. "Why won't you believe I know what I'm doing?"

"Because you don't know!"

"Well, then, give me a chance to find out, dammit!" she retorted a little wildly. "It's my body, and if I want to give it to you, then that's my own business!" She realized the absurdity of what she was saying but somehow couldn't stop the words.

Zach laughed curtly and turned away. "If all you want is a stud, Teddy, you'll have to wait until you get to Boston." He stopped as though he'd run into a wall, closing his eyes briefly as he realized what he had said to her. Behind him was utter and complete silence. "Sorry, I didn't mean that."

She said nothing.

He braced himself and turned back to face her. The only life in her white face was blazing in amber eyes, and he couldn't read the emotion burning there. "Teddy . . . I'm sorry."

She looked at him as though he were a stranger just met, her head tilted a little, the expression on her pale face vaguely curious. "You can be cruel, can't you, Zach." It wasn't a question, just a peculiarly detached observation. "As you said, if I had a brain worthy of the name, I'd be afraid of you too."

It hurt, and Zach knew he deserved it. He nodded a little, accepting it, then went over to his equipment silently and began labeling tapes, storing them neatly. Packing away unnecessary things. Getting ready, she realized, to leave this place.

Teddy finished cleaning up, moving by rote, then forced herself to do other things, to keep busy so that she couldn't think. It didn't work, but at least she wasn't feeling very much. Those wild feelings, she thought, had been shocked into stillness by this rejection, leaving only the dim echoes of what had been.

It was late in the day, and Zach had silently left the cabin several times, when Teddy ran out of things to do. She had made a stab at organizing her purse, she had straightened the tumbled clothing in her suitcases, and she had cleaned up the cabin. After preparing a supper that neither of them did justice to—and in silence—she finally shut herself in the bathroom and took a bath of sorts.

It wasn't easy, but the creativity demanded for the task at least occupied her mind. The sink was small, the water cold, the room cramped. But she managed to wash by standing naked in a battered tin washtub she'd found, soaping and rinsing methodically. She even managed to wash her hair.

She emerged finally, wearing a definitely overlarge

flannel shirt as sleepwear, her hair wrapped turban-like in a towel. Ignoring the uncommunicative expanse of Zach's broad back, she crawled into bed with her comb and brush and sat toweling her hair until most of the water was out. Then she combed the tangles from the unruly mass before brushing it steadily while it dried.

The automatic motions were soothing, and Teddy blanked her mind as much as she could. By the time her hair was dry, though, her mind wasn't the problem. Since that first burst of passion between them she had been walking an emotional high-wire, surprising herself again and again by saying and doing things she hadn't anticipated. The wild mood swings from temper to depression to a kind of aching apathy seemed unmanageable and beyond her understanding.

She wavered between hope and despair, passion and anger, determination and anguish. And now she was aware of all those feelings rising in her throat, choking her, clawing to get out after the dazed stillness of hours. She set the brush and comb on the floor and slid down under the covers, turning her face to the wall. And she realized she was chewing on a knuckle only when she felt the pain and, feeling it, bit harder, because at least she knew then why she hurt.

Zach had been aware of her every movement. He had sat and kept himself busy with packing away instruments, with listening to uninformative conversations from the house and going out to check the area, with requesting and studying data from Interpol and other data banks—all of it mindless, barely scratching the surface of his thoughts.

He kept reminding himself, over and over, of why

he had turned away from Teddy. Of why he had to.
But as the hours passed, that reasonable voice grew
weary and fainter. He stopped listening to it altogether
when he heard the quiet sounds of her bathing.

He was under control again when she came out,
but didn't dare turn and watch her. Still, he knew
she was in bed and brushing her hair. He knew
when she put the brush aside and when she lay
down in the bed.

Zach did turn then, gazing toward the bed. She
was a mass of red hair and blankets, facing the wall.
She wasn't crying, he knew. It was something worse
than tears, something that reached out in a way he
didn't understand and wrenched at him. She didn't
move or make a sound, but he felt his willpower
vanish, his control splinter. For just a moment he
sat there, unable to move for the sheer power of the
feelings battering him. His? Hers? He didn't know.

He didn't care.

Zach didn't remember crossing the room but he
must have, because he found himself sitting on the
edge of the bed. He touched her shoulder, finding it
tense, spoke her name softly. She didn't move, and
he turned her gently onto her back. She was looking
up at him with huge eyes that were dry but feverish.

His large hand closed around her wrist and pulled
her knuckles away from her mouth. Her creamy
skin was reddened and bore the marks of her teeth,
and he knew she would be bruised there tomorrow.
He lifted her hand to his own mouth, rubbing his
lips softly across her knuckles. His free hand cupped
her cheek, the thumb gently drawing her bottom lip
from between her teeth.

"Don't be kind," she told him in a voice that almost wasn't there.

His mouth twisted, and Zach bent toward her, murmuring, "I haven't got a kind bone in my body." He fitted his mouth to hers, firmly and with utter possession, his tongue diving deeply to twine with hers.

Instantly, Teddy responded, her arms going around his neck, a faint whimper escaping the molten joining of their lips. She could feel his hand slide around to the nape of her neck, drawing her up against him, and his other hand was at the small of her back. Her breasts were pressed into the hardness of his chest, and the pleasure of that alone tightened an already quivering coil of desire deep inside her. They were locked together for long moments, and her body strained instinctively to be closer, to be a part of him.

He eased her back a little so that he could unbutton her shirt, his fingers quick and sure, and she lowered her arms long enough to let the flannel slide away. She would have reached out for him again—did, in fact—but he was straightening, and Teddy felt a quick flare of pure panic.

She gasped. "If you leave me now . . ."

Darkened gray eyes were sweeping her body that the discarded shirt and tumble of blankets left bared to the waist, and he smiled just a little as he swiftly unbuttoned his shirt. "No, honey," he said in a voice like rough velvet, "I'm not leaving you."

Reassured as much by the expression in his eyes as by the words, Teddy allowed her body to relax and lay still, watching him. Completely unselfconscious and utterly fascinated, she watched the golden light play over his rippling muscles, and when he bent to discard the light moccasins he always wore, she reached out to gently touch one of the several faint

ZACH'S LAW · 79

scars on his back. His muscles moved like a living
animal under her fingers, and he turned his head to
look at her with a hint of that untamed intensity in
his eyes.

"So much hurt," she murmured, thinking of mangled cougars and wounded warriors. Her fingers
traced the puckered scar that had to have been left
by a bullet, then trailed downward to follow the
curving ridge of scar tissue high on his rib cage;
God only knew what had made that awful wound.

Her hand fell away when he stood up to finish
undressing, and she caught her breath. The raw male
beauty of him made her ache, heart and soul, and
the vital force he exuded ignited her senses instantly.
His big body was tanned flesh covering corded muscle; the smooth expanse of bronze was broken only
by the jet-black hair lightly furring his long legs,
covering his powerful chest, and arrowing down his
flat stomach to the thicket over his loins.

Clothed, he was an imposing man, the size and
obvious strength of him intimidating, his grace of
movement riveting; naked, he was all that and more.
He was a male animal in the prime of his power and
virility, and he was beautiful.

Teddy reached out to him when he swept the covers away and lowered his weight beside her, but he
caught her wrists gently in one big hand and an-
chored them to the pillow above her head. "I want to
look at you." His voice was a deep, soft rumble. He
gazed down at her slender body, which seemed curiously insubstantial because it was half hidden in
his own shadow.

Her breasts rose and fell quickly with her shallow
breathing, the position of her arms lifting and
rounding them so that they begged mutely to be

touched, kissed. She seemed incredibly fragile, her body delicate, her creamy flesh the kind that would be easily bruised; but she was unmarked, utterly perfect, and beautifully feminine.

Zach swallowed hard, but it didn't ease the ache in his throat. He felt a dizzying, savage wave of desire surge through his body, a driving need to possess, to feel her body sheathing his.

"Zach?" Her voice was a whisper, her eyes not frightened but wide and feverish.

He bent his head and kissed her, exploring the dark sweetness of her mouth, and he felt the heat of her response increase instantly when his free hand surrounded the thrusting curve of her breast. He could feel the hard arousal of her nipple against his palm, and when his fingers tugged gently at the coral bud, her body arched instinctively and a kittenlike sound tangled in her throat.

His lips trailed down her neck and across her breastbone, hot and shaking, until they closed over a nipple and drew it strongly into his mouth.

Teddy bit her lip, her eyes half closed, the storm descending on her for a second time. But now there was not even minimal control, and she had no idea of what the crescendo of this violence would do to her. It seemed she'd be torn apart, waves of pleasure battering her, and she found the breath somewhere to voice the single doubt in her mind.

"I feel—I can't control it, what you make me feel. It frightens me—"

He raised his head for a moment, gray eyes shimmering hotly, then kissed her lips with a hunger only just tempered with gentleness. "Don't be afraid," he murmured huskily. "Don't ever be afraid of this."

As his head lifted again, Teddy felt his hand slide

down over her quivering belly, and even as the muscles of her thighs relaxed and responded to his insistent touch, she was aware of another tension, deeper inside her, tautly coiled and waiting for something. Something . . .

She cried out in surprise and pleasure, her body arching again, when his knowing fingers combed among the red curls and found the slick heat awaiting him there. Shock waves of delight swept over her, and she didn't worry about control anymore, didn't worry that there was something unnatural in the wildness of what she felt.

He held her trapped, her arms above her head, one of his legs between hers; she felt helpless and yet safe, safe if he'd only hold on to her, because she couldn't hold on to herself anymore.

"Don't let go of me," she whispered wildly, feeling that she'd float away somewhere if he didn't hold her down, anchor her somehow.

"I won't," he promised thickly. And he didn't let go until he rose above, slipping between her legs and bracing himself over her. She caught at his shoulders then, feeling the smooth hardness of his hips against her inner thighs and a gentle probing of the aching flesh between.

Her remaining breath caught in her throat and she stared up at his face, in that instant imprinting his features deep in her soul for all time. She felt her flesh stretching to admit him, and a tiny pain brought instinctive tension.

Zach made a rough sound and lowered his head to give her a kiss that was both gentle and fierce. "I'll hurt you," he warned in a hoarse, raw tone. "Just for a moment."

Aware suddenly of the rigid tension of his muscles, Teddy knew then what it was costing him to hold back for her sake, and tension dissolved in a warm flood of trust. Her arms coiled around his neck, and she lifted her head to kiss him, murmuring wordlessly.

He groaned, a shudder rippling through his big body. His breathing seemed tortured, ripped from his chest with harsh sounds, and she could see the pulse hammering in his throat. He moved with shattering care, hesitating when she gasped, catching her faint cry with his savagely tender kiss.

The pain had been sharp but brief, and Teddy forgot it instantly. Wonderingly, she absorbed the incredible sensations of joining, the stark power of him, the alien fullness her body welcomed with its own heat. His flesh sank deeply into hers in a merging so complete and utterly perfect that she felt a part of him and gloried in the feeling.

"Teddy . . . ?"

She opened her eyes, realizing only then that they had closed, and looked up at him. Her arms tightened around the strong column of his neck and she moved against him, drawing another groan from him.

The velvety clasp of her body sent a wild shiver of pleasure up his spine, and the soft, unconscious sounds she made drove him crazy with need. He moved slowly at first, but soon her body was lifting to meet his thrusts and the heat of her scalded him, drove him still wilder. The innate fire of her passion increased his own, building it higher and higher until his hunger for her was a living thing consuming him alive.

Teddy was writhing beneath him, and he lost all control over his own body. Some distant part of his mind told him he was being too rough, but he heard nothing except for the howling of intolerable need. He couldn't get enough of her, couldn't sate his starving senses or satisfy the terrible craving.

And even as the hot explosion of her ecstasy caught him in its violent shock waves, even as their mindless cries were strangled in a fierce kiss of devastating completion, there was another explosion deep inside Zach.

Buried somewhere near the core of his being, the iron bars of a cage burst outward with the wild force of the emotions swirling around it. And he knew dimly and with utter certainty that he was vulnerable now to her, knew that all the strength he could command would never be able to stand against her.

He had fallen into another trap, and this one promised to tear the heart out of him.

Five

The turbulent storm had passed, leaving exhausted peace in its wake, and this time Teddy didn't fear the return of it. It would return, she knew, in all its wild power every time Zach touched her.

Her body was utterly limp and she couldn't find the strength to open her eyes, but she managed a faint protest when the warmth of his body left her.

"Shhh," he murmured. "I'll be right back."

Teddy heard the click of the lamp and sensed more than saw darkness fill the cabin. And she heard other faint sounds that puzzled her slightly, until Zach returned to her. He sat on the edge of the bed and bent to kiss her, gently parting her legs and pressing a cool, damp cloth between them, caring for her with shattering tenderness.

Then he was beside her, drawing the blankets up around them and pulling her close. Teddy nestled against his hard side in warm contentment.

"I'm sorry I hurt you," he told her huskily, his lips moving in her hair.

"You hardly did," she murmured truthfully. And then, because she had to, she said, "I love you, Zach."

For a moment he went still, even his heart seeming to stop, then his arm tightened around her. "Mine," he rasped almost inaudibly. "For now, at least."

Teddy opened her eyes in the darkness, troubled. Not because he had made no declaration of love; she'd not expected one. But because she thought that just so would he have spoken of something priceless and yearned for that he was allowed to hold for only a moment.

"Zach—"

"Go to sleep, honey."

"I'm not sleepy," she protested. And it was true. She was weary but wide-awake. And though she sensed that her warrior's armor lay around him in shards, she was suddenly afraid that the morning would find him securely within it once more. She might have only this night to make a place for herself near his heart, and she had to *try*.

"You should be sleepy," he told her.

"Are you?" she countered.

Zach sighed softly. "No."

"Then talk to me. Tell me . . . tell me about your work and your friends."

His hand moved over her back in a stroking motion, gentle and slow, and after a moment he began talking. At first, unused to exposing his emotions aloud, he spoke in short, stark sentences, revealing only facts. But gradually, as if a dam somewhere inside him had been breached, he revealed more of himself in talking of his life. In the dark intimacy of their bed he tentatively and at first awkwardly gave her the gift of himself.

Teddy nearly held her breath as she listened, fearful that he would realize what he was doing and, realizing, stop. She listened as he spoke briefly of his Army days, mentioning them only because it was there he began to learn electronics. Listened as he talked about meeting Joshua Long when both were young in years but old and tough in experience. Listened as simple words revealed a friendship that had weathered more than fifteen years and explosions both personal and professional.

She saw in her mind the circle of Zach's trust and watched and listened as others entered it after Josh Long, their places won by time and events. She saw a cheerful and charming blond man, Lucas Kendrick; a deceptively lazy attorney, Rafferty Lewis; and she saw the two women who had won places within that circle with their own brands of courage and strength and honesty.

She listened to her warrior make light of his own part in various battles, and she ached inside because his life had taught him so well to guard himself.

He was letting her in, but the cabin was dark and still, and she didn't know what the morning would bring. What he was giving of himself he could never reclaim, she knew, but she also knew that the knowledge could well be all she was left with.

And she held on to him tightly, silently vowing that she would find the strength and courage to fight for him, for his love. And that she would somehow find the knowledge she needed to convince him that her love was real.

"No family?" she asked quietly.

"No. Raised in foster homes."

Teddy rubbed her cheek against his chest, aching for him. "I love you," she murmured.

He turned her face up and kissed her gently. "Go to sleep," he whispered, and this time she did, still holding him tightly in an effort to keep some part of him.

She awoke the instant he began drawing away, knowing that it was morning even though the cabin was still dark. "Zach?"

He paused a moment to kiss her but still drew away and slid from the bed. "Go back to sleep," he told her. "It's barely dawn."

Instead, Teddy raised herself up on her elbows and rubbed her dry eyes automatically, waiting for the light. Her body felt different. Vaguely sore but not really painful, and curiously more alive than ever before. She blinked when the lamp came on, and when her eyes cleared, her first sight was of Zach's magnificent naked body.

He was completely unselfconscious and unconcerned by his nudity as he padded silently over to his equipment shelf to check for activity gone unheard in the night, and Teddy's mouth went dry at the riveting sight of him. She could feel the faint rumble of her inner storm and relished the return of it. But she was also anxious, half afraid he had withdrawn from her more than just physically.

She threw back the covers and slid out of bed, unconscious of her own nakedness until he turned his head to look at her. She went very still, gazing at his immobile face, searching for some sign of what he was thinking or feeling.

Very quietly he said, "You are beautiful."

Teddy was startled, unnerved. "No," she said honestly, "I'm not."

His eyes flared. "You are." And she was. Her vibrant hair tumbled around her shoulders like flame, its color and silky mass emphasizing the delicate, vital face and huge satin eyes. Her naked body was slender and utterly feminine, her small breasts perfectly shaped, her waist tiny and hips curved. And, surprisingly, the tempestuous passion he had shared with her had left no marks on her creamy flesh.

Zach crossed the room to her, his tread the soundless padding of a jungle predator. When he reached her, his hands found her waist, drawing her against him, and she came into his arms eagerly.

"I'm not beautiful," she murmured when she could, delighting in the sensuous rasp of his morning beard against her skin. "But I'm so glad you think I am."

He half closed his eyes, his hands slipping down over her hips, fitting her more tightly against his own awakening body. A bit hoarsely, he said, "You drive me crazy, and I can't keep my hands off you."

"Good," she whispered.

He was kissing her, each kiss more fierce and possessive than the last. "Not good," he said deeply. "You need time, honey, you'll be sore—"

She looked up at him with the slightly wild eyes of rising passion, and her voice was fierce. "If you think *that's* going to stop me—!"

He was almost laughing when he eased her back onto the bed, exhilarated by her uninhibited desire. She was wild in loving him, and he forgot everything but her.

They had dressed and eaten breakfast, when a

conversation from the house drew Zach's attention to the recorders. He went to listen while Teddy cleared the table and cleaned up, and by the time she was finished, so was the conversation.

"Anything important?"

He was frowning a little. "They're leaving again. I think I'll check out the goods one more time."

"You're still bothered by something."

"Something too vague to put my finger on," he said. He crossed the space between them and framed most of her face in one big hand, lifting her chin and kissing her. He raised his head at last, looking down at her for a long, long moment, his thumb rubbing gently across the lips still swollen from earlier kisses. "You belong to me," he said in a strange, suspended voice.

"Yes," she said instantly, knowing she did, knowing she was his, body and soul, no matter what the future held.

He enfolded her in his arms and held her tightly for a moment. "I won't let anything happen to you," he said firmly, and it was a promise, a vow chiseled from stone.

"I know." She hugged as much of him as she could, but released him instantly when he stepped back.

Zach drew on his shoulder harness, automatically and methodically checking the big silver automatic. "I'll probably be gone for quite a while," he said. "This may be my last chance to look things over before they ship out."

"All right."

The door closed softly behind him.

Teddy stood perfectly still for a long time, staring

at that door. A chill was playing up and down her spine, and a sudden fear clenched her heart.

"I wont let anything happen to you."

Why, she wondered, had he said what he did just then? Had some Scottish forebear of his own gifted Zach with a presentiment of danger? There had always been danger, of course, but why did she feel now as though it were much closer and far more deadly?

She gasped suddenly as a dizzying wave broke over her, only dimly surprised that she was somehow being granted a second gift of vision. The image flashed with lightning swiftness, and a moan broke from her lips in a sound of anguish.

No. No, it wouldn't happen. . . .

The image was gone, and she was left staring at the closed door. Vaguely, she wondered at the arguments that it was possible, given knowledge, to change the future. Either she had been given two differing glimpses of the future, or else . . . or else both would take place. Unless she could somehow change at least one of them.

There really was no choice for her.

She found herself standing before the computer, and sat down quickly. She turned the machine on, her thoughts centered on the man who meant more to her than her own life.

"Forgive me, Zach," she whispered into the silence of the cabin. "I have to do *something*. . . ."

Her fingers were steady and sure on the keys, and her brow furrowed as she concentrated intensely on remembering the sequence. Swiftly, she typed out the proper access codes.

•   •   •

An hour passed, and Teddy paced the cabin. The computer had been off for half of that time, and her nerves had stretched to the screaming point. She was no longer thinking of what she had done, that was past and unregretted.

She thought instead of what had driven her to it. She had wondered, in the beginning, how people survived the awful ache of love, and Zach's physical possession, though blunting the pain, had left the yearning intact. She thought she would never lose that, even if Zach one day learned to love and trust her completely. The thought of it held no terrors for her.

But what *did* terrify her was the possibility that Zach would go forever beyond her reach, leaving only the terrible anguish of knowing just a part of his love. If he sent her away, or walked away himself, at least there was the belief that she would somehow be able to hold him in her arms again. But if he were taken from her by an act of violence—

She frowned a little, something nagging at her. After a brief hesitation she went over to kneel by her luggage and purse. A moment's digging brought out the case of tranquilizer darts that Zach had returned to her purse. She held it thoughtfully, then scrabbled through the luggage he hadn't bothered to check in the beginning. The dart pistol was just where she'd packed it.

Acting on nothing but the need to be prepared, she readied two darts and loaded the pistol, then put it and the case in her purse. Then she carried the purse to the table and left it there before beginning to pace again.

God only knew if she'd have reason—or a chance— to use the pistol, but having it ready made her feel just a bit less helpless. And she was an accurate shot, there was that.

The pacing didn't help and she stopped, swearing softly.

Teddy shivered, hugging herself for a warmth that never came. She was wearing jeans and a flannel shirt of Zach's that swallowed her but bore the faint musky scent of him. And she was afraid.

She was desperately afraid.

When the first shot came, she literally jerked under the emotional impact of it. Then she stood frozen, hearing the second shot and the third. Before the last echoes had died away, she was tugging open the door and running, completely forgetting the pistol in her purse. Half a dozen steps from the cabin door she paused, looking around in an effort to get her bearings. Impenetrable forest surrounded her, but a fourth gunshot jerked her to the right and sent her racing, only one thought, one agonized question in her mind.

She hadn't realized they were so close, and burst through into the clearing surrounding the house without being able to stop herself. Immediately a whining bullet chipped bark from the tree to her left, and from her right, rising with a crash from the undergrowth, lunged Zach.

Between one heartbeat and the next, Teddy knew with haunting despair that she herself had blindly invited the reality of the image she had seen with such distortion. With every fiber of her being she had known that Zach could take care of himself, would be canny and cautious, but that he would instantly and without thought shield her with his own body from danger, yet she had rashly placed herself in just that position.

A sharp report and the hollow thud of a bullet striking flesh, and scarlet blood . . .

If only she had remained in the cabin.

And in that instant, between one heartbeat and the next, she twisted violently in an irrevocable attempt to change what had to be.

Her lightning movement threw Zach off-balance, and he, too, was twisting in midair, reaching out for her, a raw, despairing terror tightening the muscles of his face. And he almost got her, his outstretched hand reaching her arm. But he jerked her around before he pulled her down with him, and when her back was to the house, in that fleeting second another shot rang out.

Zach wasted no time. With an arm around her waist he hauled her back into the undergrowth, his big automatic bucking in his hand. The sound of it was deafening as he fired behind them and tried to pin down the gunman. Then the house was lost from sight, and he lifted her into his arms and carried her swiftly through the woods toward the cabin.

"What the *hell* are you doing out here?" he demanded in a furious, shaking voice. "Dammit, Teddy, you could have been killed!"

"I was worried about you," she said very softly, staring up at his white face.

He said something violently explicit between gritted teeth.

She had left the door open, and Zach carried her inside and set her on her feet, reaching back to slam it shut behind them. "We've got a few minutes at least," he said, still angry. "I winged the bastard just before you came diving into it, so I doubt he'll come hunting us in a hurry—"

Teddy felt very peculiar. She was cold and couldn't seem to feel the floor beneath her feet, and the most appalling weakness was spreading throughout her body. *Shock,* she realized vaguely. *I'm in shock.* She looked down at the floor as the sound of the door slamming shook the cabin, and bemusedly watched tiny splashes of scarlet color the rough wooden planking beside her boots, and she idly wondered why her fingers were red, too, and why her arm was so heavy and why Zach's voice seemed to be fading into the depths of some bottomless cave . . .

"*Teddy!*"

He caught her as she swayed, lifted her, and carried her to the bed where he covered her with blankets. When she opened her eyes, Zach was ripping her left sleeve from cuff to shoulder. He swore steadily in an odd monotone and seemed a bit clumsy when he hurried to get the first-aid kit. Teddy thought about that from the distant reaches of her vast detachment.

Zach wasn't clumsy.

How odd.

She came back to herself with a painful suddenness that made her gasp. Her arm was still heavy, but now it throbbed with fire and she could see why when she looked at it. The gauze Zach was using to wipe her skin was stained bright red, and there was an ugly gash that ran from her elbow almost to her shoulder. Fascinated in a horrified way, she saw that the bullet had torn into her sleeve just above the elbow, plowed a furrow up her arm, and torn its way out at her shoulder.

She remembered the moment she'd been shot. She had been off-balance, yanked around by Zach's lunge, her arm thrown up. She remembered the burning sensation in her arm, barely noticed at the time. And she realized that if she had not jerked backward and twisted, if Zach had not been forced to twist his own body in order to reach her, he would have caught the bullet squarely in the center of his back.

It almost made the pain go away.

Trying to shake off the weakness of lost blood and shock, she murmured, "I'm fine, Zach. It's just a scratch."

He sent her one look from glittering gray eyes, then concentrated entirely on the task of cleaning and bandaging her wound. His face was ashen, the scar on his cheek a livid slash, and his hands trembled slightly.

Teddy wouldn't have willingly put him through this for anything she could think of, but her heart leaped in joy when she realized that he really did care about her, whether he knew it or not. He had seen uncounted battlefield wounds and had suffered a few himself, yet the sight of what was in all honesty a slight injury to her had shaken him badly.

In silence, he cleaned and disinfected the wound, being amazingly gentle under the circumstances, then bandaged it very carefully. Teddy found that the pain was only a dull throb, although she had no idea how badly it might hurt when the shock wore off completely.

"It didn't harm anything vital," she said finally, watching his face.

"No," he agreed. "But you . . . lost a lot of blood."

Trying to ease the pain revealed by his bleak look, she said, "Only a pint or so. I've given that much at the blood bank."

"Not in shock, you haven't. And not because of a

bullet." His expression remained the same, but now Teddy could tell that something terrible was going on inside Zach. He was holding her arm in his hands, staring down at the neat white bandage, and his long fingers quivered. In a strange, wondering tone, he said, "The bastard shot you."

Teddy caught her breath, staring at him, as aware of the danger filling the small cabin as if it were a visible thing. Menace literally came off Zach in waves, cold and deadly, like an Arctic wind howling off a glacier.

In the back of her mind, memory stirred, and she recalled something a psychologist friend had once told her. One man in perhaps ten thousand was a throwback to those old Scandinavian berserkers, whose blood rages had been awesome and uncontrollable; that such a man, pushed too far, became something more dangerous than any man-made weapon could ever be. On those rare occasions he was beyond rational thought, existing briefly in an icy, remote place where violent action was the only solution to inner rage and anguish.

Zach was going back up to the house, she realized. In a blind, murderous rage, he was going after the man who had shot her. And there wouldn't be any caution this time. He was a ticking time bomb, and the dear Lord only knew what would be destroyed by the explosion.

Teddy gazed at him, at his still, white face and blank eyes, seeing his muscles bunch in preparation for action, and she rolled the dice one more time. If she had reached him, if he *did* care for her deeply enough . . .

"Zach?" Her voice was calm and soft, nothing in it

indicating that she was attempting to call a man back from hell.

After an agonizingly long moment he looked at her, and the blind glaze slowly left his eyes. His muscles gradually relaxed, the tension seeped away. And he was there, he was sane. On a rough sigh he murmured, "Teddy."

She was enormously relieved and deeply shaken. She had hoped to coax a wild wolf to walk by her side, but she had never even dared to dream that the mere sound of her voice calling his name could keep him from tearing out the throat of a mortal enemy.

And she wondered if the fool in the house would ever know just how close to death he had come.

Gesturing to the arm he was still holding gently, she said, "I can hardly feel it."

After a moment Zach lowered her arm. He got up and went over to her luggage, moving gracefully again, and bent to rummage among her clothing. "You'll have to dress warmly. There isn't any heat where we're going."

She watched him. "Where are we going?"

"A little farther up the mountain. That stuff's coming in tomorrow, and Ryan's not about to let me or anyone else end his career without a hell of a fight; as soon as his men return, he'll be coming here after us."

"You know him," she said, surprised. "I mean, personally."

Zach returned to the bed with one of her flannel shirts and a thick sweater. He sat beside her and began getting her out of the torn and bloody shirt she was wearing. "I know him," he admitted. "We tangled a few years ago when he tried his hand at a little industrial sabotage."

"Did you know he was here? I mean—"

He shook his head. "No. But I know now what was eating at me before. I heard three voices, and only three have been recorded on the tapes. What bothered me was that none of the three sounded like the leader, and yet he seemed to be nearby. Ryan was there in the house all the time; one of his little habits is that he never speaks when he's in a house or car and possibly under observation or electronic surveillance—when he's on a job, that is. He's careful. Very careful."

"So when you went to the house earlier—"

"For once he hadn't left with his men. And since I've been listening more than watching, I never knew there were four men in the house." Zach slid her injured arm gently into the sleeve of the flannel shirt and began buttoning it. "Damn Hagen. *That* is what he so conveniently forgot to tell me that Clay Ryan was the ringleader of the bunch. No wonder he was so insistent that I was the only one who could do this job."

"Why?" Her voice was briefly muffled as he pulled the sweater over her head, then emerged clearly. "Because you'd caught this Ryan before?"

It seemed at first that Zach wasn't going to answer. He eased her arms through the sleeves of the sweater and then settled the ribbed hem around her hips with a smoothing movement that was almost a caress. She was sitting up easily, apparently bothered little by weakness, but she was pale, and Zach knew that she *was* weakened by shock and the loss of blood.

It hurt him to see her like that.

He got up and went to efficiently gather together what they would need, stowing blankets and food in a duffel bag, rolling up the sleeping bag, and selecting ammunition for his handgun and rifle.

"Zach?" she prompted.

Packing away the tapes he'd made from conversations in the house, Zach finally answered in a conversational tone that attempted to lessen the effect of what he was saying.

"Clay Ryan is at the top of the FBI's list and has been for ten years. He's done everything from robbery on a large scale through blackmail, sabotage, gunrunning, arson, terrorist activities, and murder. And he's very good at each of them. Each job is different and handled differently; he considers his hired thugs disposable, and they never even know his name; his M.O. changes from job to job, and he never repeats himself.

"He's never seen the inside of a prison. In fact, he has never been arrested on any charge and has never even been held for questioning. There's never been proof enough against him for any of that, and whenever probable cause *could* be found to pull him in, he'd always disappeared without a trace. Until the next job. And, to date, only one living witness can claim to have seen him actually perform a criminal act."

"You," she said hollowly, knowing it was true.

Zach was methodically reloading the clip of his automatic and didn't look up. "Me," he confirmed mildly. "That sabotage I mentioned. He destroyed six months' work in a computer-design laboratory. And he got away. The company belonged to Josh. I managed to track him down just as he was setting explosives to torch an import company that also belonged to Josh. Ryan had been paid a fortune by a competitor to cause heavy losses to Long Enterprises."

"What happened?"

"The import company didn't blow." Zach's voice was calm. "But some of the explosives did, before I could get my hands on him. The blast put me in the hospital and should have killed him. Even though he vanished, the FBI didn't believe he was dead any more than I did; they kept him on their list."

Teddy remembered the curving scar on his rib cage and thought she knew now how that had happened. "And you think Hagen knew all that? And knew Ryan was involved here when he sent you?"

"Of course he knew. Hagen likes to believe he knows everything. He doesn't, but he often knows too damned much. He talked me into this because he knows I hate gunrunners; you can bet he was saving Ryan's identity as an ace up his sleeve in case I needed a little extra incentive."

Teddy watched as he shrugged into his quilted flannel jacket, then said quietly, "You don't like it when someone goes after something you feel responsible for, do you?" She was thinking of Zach's reaction when a kidnapped lady was snatched from inside one of his security systems, and of his tracking down Ryan when one of Josh Long's companies had been damaged.

He looked at her. "No," he said flatly. "I don't."

She felt a chill and tried to keep the reaction from showing on her face. Were Zach's feelings for her and his grim desire to protect her the product of a sense of responsibility? Only that? she wondered.

No. No, it was more. She knew it was more. Because if it *wasn't* more, how could she have called him back from that awful place his rage had sent him to? How could she have reached him there if he hadn't opened up some part of himself to her?

She held on tightly to that knowledge.

With everything packed and ready, Zach coolly and efficiently disabled the computer by wiping the hard disc clean and cutting the connections to the batteries and phone lines. "We'll have to leave your stuff," he told her, gathering the rifle and bags. "It won't be for long, though, and with any luck, Ryan won't bother with it."

When he came back to her, Teddy realized what he was going to do. "Zach, I can walk! You're carrying everything else."

Without a word he bent and lifted her easily into his arms.

She looked at everything he was carrying over his shoulders or on his back, then sighed and put her uninjured arm around his neck. "We're going to have to have a long discussion about these macho instincts of yours," she told him, but not as if the instincts in question bothered her very much.

"Right."

"Oh—and my purse."

Faint amusement lightened his expression. "Afraid you may have to leash a rabid Doberman?"

"You never know," she murmured, reaching to snag her purse from the table as they passed.

He carried her out of the cabin.

Teddy didn't pay too much attention to where he was carrying her, although she knew he was heading away from the house and to higher ground. Instead, she gazed steadily at his strong face and asked the question that had been flitting in and out of her mind since the previous night.

"Zach? What changed your mind?" When he

glanced down at her quizzically, she elaborated, "You were so determined that we wouldn't be lovers. What changed your mind?"

Showing no strain because of his burdens, he walked on a few steps in silence before replying. Finally, somewhat remotely, he said, "My mind didn't change. You'd tempt a saint beyond bearing, Teddy."

"Hey, pal, I'm no siren," she managed to say lightly.

He looked down at her for an instant, and something savage and utterly male flared hotly in his eyes. Then it was gone, and his voice remained almost imperceptibly distant. "Call it chemistry, then. Or biology. Hell, call it lust."

If Teddy had believed that *he* believed what he was saying, she would have been deeply hurt. But she didn't believe him.

He was back in his warrior's armor again.

And she didn't try to crawl in there with him, not this time. If she had learned anything by now, she had learned that they were in a jungle with a predator at their backs and danger all around. His armor would protect him, and that was more important to her than an admission of caring that never could be forced out of him, anyway.

She put her head on his shoulder and closed her eyes.

They were two hundred yards from the cabin, and a great deal higher, when Zach finally stopped. He stood gazing down the mountainside for a moment. The house was visible below, looking unthreatening, no cars in the drive, no movement. Ryan had clearly decided to wait for reinforcements before going after them.

Zach couldn't have said why he knew that Ryan intended to go on with his plans and ship the valuables, but he was certain that that was the case. He was also certain that when Ryan and his men found the cabin deserted, the leader would not hesitate to begin combing the mountain for them.

In Ryan's place, most men would assume that Zach had cleared out to get reinforcements of his own and would therefore hasten to clear out themselves. But Clay Ryan wasn't most men, and Zach didn't think he'd make that assumption.

In a curious way, Zach believed there was some thread of similarity between him and the other man, that they somehow understood each other despite meeting face-to-face only twice and under violent circumstances—or maybe because of that. There was strong personal enmity between them: To Ryan, Zach was the man who had seen his face and cost him a lucrative commission; to Zach, Ryan was the dangling thread, the one that got away.

This was between just the two of them.

So Ryan, Zach thought, would not assume. He would go on with his plans, confident that he would be able to deal with the threat posed by Zach's presence.

Hardly feeling the weight in his arms but very aware of her warm body, Zach looked down at Teddy's sleeping face. She looked so young. *Was* so young. Ten years separated them, and yet Zach felt immeasurably older.

She had become important to him, and Zach hadn't meant to let that happen. He accepted the feelings, but the guarded part of him refused to voice them aloud. Because he still believed that when this was over, when the danger was past, she would discover that her feelings had been temporary, or even unreal.

And it would destroy him to see the lack of love in her eyes.

It would, he realized hollowly, probably destroy him, anyway. When he sent her away, he'd be tearing his own heart out.

"Zach?" Her voice was sleepy, her eyes blurred when she looked up at him questioningly.

His arms tightened around her, and Zach glanced behind him at the hollowed-out area of the hillside that was not quite a cave. The Jeep was a mile away and well hidden; he had no intention of going anywhere near it until they were ready to leave this place for good.

So, for now, this was home.

He bent to place her carefully on a bed of moss. "We'll stay here, honey," he murmured, and wondered how much longer he would be able to hear the magic of her voice saying his name.

Six

Teddy slept for most of the day, and Zach knew it was the best thing for her after being wounded. He had unrolled the sleeping bag inside their hollowed-out resting place and tucked her within it before doing anything else. Her eyes opened drowsily from time to time, but once she saw him near, she would relax into sleep again.

Zach kept busy. He stowed all their supplies near the sleeping bag and then used sticks and brush to narrow the opening of their cavelet; they were downwind of the house, and he had hopes of being able to build a fire later if he could hide the light of it from the house.

He watched the house throughout the afternoon. When Ryan's men returned and quickly found the cabin, Zach felt somewhat apprehensive. He had been right, though, because the men made no effort to comb the surrounding area and promptly returned to the main house.

Teddy was deeply asleep, so Zach left the cavelet

late in the afternoon to rig a few early-warning devices around the perimeter. He wasn't overly concerned that Ryan and his men would come looking, but even though Zach had never been a Boy Scout, he fully appreciated the virtue of always being prepared for the unexpected.

If he had been another kind of man, Zach would have taken Teddy and left the area, summoning help or at least a relief to take over his job. But it was against his very nature to leave a job unfinished, particularly when in doing so, he would be asking another man to face a danger he himself chose to avoid. He couldn't do that. He had deliberately lied to his friends in order to make certain they wouldn't get involved in another of Hagen's infamous assignments, and he wasn't about to ask anyone else to do so. And there was still a chance he could pull this off. Hagen had promised—whatever *that* was worth—that he could have a squad of federal marshals up here within an hour to arrest the gang once Zach obtained proof that the stolen artwork was at the house. He had that proof, in the form of photos and recordings, but nothing specifically linked Ryan to the thefts and resales.

Zach wondered if Hagen had realized he would eventually discover Ryan's presence and be forced to alter the initial plan. Of course he had known, and probably planned to tell Zach when he called to summon the marshals. It had to be Ryan the federal man was really after, and far better to catch the criminal in the act of trading stolen artwork for illegal guns than merely in possession of the art.

And there was the rest of the mess. In order to arrest the men who would receive the artwork in exchange for guns, it would be necessary to allow the shipment to leave as planned, and to trace it to its delivery point. They knew where the guns were being stored and where they'd come from, but it had been impossible to find out who had bought them; the actual trade was necessary to establish that connection.

If Ryan accompanied the shipment, presumably and logically to oversee the trade and examine the guns, he could be caught then—but would he? Would he take the chance of being caught in transit with stolen artwork—especially now that he knew Zach was nearby and likely trying to catch him in just such a position? And would the men who had purchased the guns allow themselves to risk the possibility of being caught near the stolen goods *and* the illegally purchased guns?

Or would everybody involved send middlemen for that?

It seemed to Zach, brooding over the whole thing as he set a few trip wires and snares, that entirely too much would be taken on trust unless all parties *did* meet face-to-face before or during the trade. And in Zach's experience, very few on either side of the law were that trusting. Unless each saw his goods before the trade, how were they to know they were receiving what had been promised?

The guns, under surveillance now by at least one other agent, had been stored at an old disused munitions dump in the mountains west of Pueblo. Not the easiest place, certainly, from which to ship guns out of the country without a great deal of risk. And since the men they believed responsible for purchasing the guns lived in the East, there was also the problem of getting the artwork safely back there without incident.

Mentally, Zach constructed a rough plan to deal with as much as he could given his limited knowledge. When the goods left here, he could alert Hagen; whether or not Ryan left with the shipment, he might or might not take his men along, so they could be picked up by the marshals if he disbanded the group. Then Zach could follow the shipment along its route either to where the guns waited or else to some transfer point midway.

And then . . . and then what? His next actions, Zach realized, would depend on what happened then. Or what didn't happen.

It was a hell of a rotten plan, he realized in disgust, with far too many things left to chance, and far, far too much he didn't know.

Just Hagen's style.

"I caught you off guard. Hardly professional of you, my boy."

"What the hell are you doing here?" His tone was irritated and hardly respectful, and Kelsey was scowling somewhat ferociously as he holstered his automatic and glared at the decidedly unwelcome post-midnight visitor.

Hagen came around a stack of wooden crates, his corpulent form moving with unexpected grace and silence as he reached the circle of faint light in which his agent stood. He was, as usual, dressed in a business suit that was straining at the seams, his bum's hat perched on his head. Not a fleck of dust marred the shine of his shoes.

Ignoring Kelsey's demand, he asked casually, "What have you done with the guards?" His tone implied that he confidently expected Kelsey to tell him that twenty desperadoes were bound and gagged in a dark corner somewhere.

Kelsey snorted. "What guards? I moved around this place like a shadow for two days until I realized not a soul had been left on guard here. And no security devices, either." He ran a hand through his thick hair and frowned at his boss. "You didn't answer me. What're you doing here?"

Hagen was gazing around at the considerable number of stacked crates. "A slight change in plans, my boy."

Wincing, Kelsey muttered, "Oh, my God," as one who had learned to beware that simple phrase.

Hagen's cherubic face remained bland. "An unanticipated player has entered the game."

Kelsey stared at him for a moment, then grinned abruptly. "Don't tell me. That human element you were so sure you'd avoided this time? You sent Zach out alone to the back of beyond, only bad guys for company, and fate threw a wild card into his hand?"

"Colorful metaphors," Hagen noted, somewhat reluctantly approving. He sighed. "These men appear to have a penchant for conducting romances at the most unlikely times."

The men he referred to, Kelsey knew, were the reluctant agents drafted by Hagen months before, when they had stumbled onto one of his operations. Josh Long, Zach Steele, Rafferty Lewis, and Lucas Kendrick were a close-knit bunch with a habit of looking out for one another, and shared an uncanny ability to jolt Hagen out of his normally unshakable composure.

Kelsey enjoyed watching that, no matter how many times plans had to be revised because of it. It wasn't often that anyone got the better of the boss. But this time even he was startled by Hagen's observation.

"Romance? You mean, Zach managed to find a woman way out there? How on earth—"

"I don't know, but he destroyed her car." Hagen sounded disgusted, unusually emotional. "And Sarah Lewis came asking questions. Raven and her bothersome husband flew back from Canada last night ahead of schedule, and Rafferty Lewis somehow managed to acquire an army helicopter this afternoon. No doubt he made use of Josh Long's military contacts—not that *they* would ever admit it, of course."

"What's Lucas done?" Kelsey murmured.

Hagen glared at him. "You mean, aside from going to Boston in order to reassure the girl's sister that she was fine? Oh, not much. Except that he's used his intelligence contacts to find out that Ryan is the one we're after." Parenthetically and in a tone that boded ill for someone, he added, "I'm going to plug *that* leak."

"Well," Kelsey said, "it looks like the gang—excepting Sarah, since she wouldn't risk the baby—is about to be all here." He shook his head in mild disgust. "Boss, you really should have known that if you brought *one* of that group in, you'd get them all."

If Kelsey had been looking, he would have seen a tiny smile curve Hagen's bow-shaped mouth; when he did look, however, all he saw was a disgruntled cherub.

"A change in plans," Hagen repeated.

Kelsey groaned.

Teddy was sitting just inside the cavelet, her arms

around her raised knees, when Zach returned. Looking wide-awake and largely recovered from her injury, she got to her feet as he came in, and if her arm seemed a bit stiff, at least she didn't hesitate to use it.

"We can see the house from here," she said.

Zach looked at her searchingly, and the tight feeling in his chest gradually eased. She was going to be all right, he realized. For a while he hadn't let himself believe that. He nodded in response to her comment. "We can see it. If the men inside have a pair of binoculars, they can see us as well."

"I thought we were hiding."

"No. We've just found a more defensible position where we can't be surprised."

Teddy thought about that, watching as Zach dropped an armload of small sticks and branches inside the cavelet and knelt to start a fire. The sun was going down, and it was gradually getting dark.

She remembered that Zach had approached obliquely, holding to cover whenever possible. She studied the way he had narrowed the cavelet's entrance, noting that he was building the fire behind the shield of branches so it would be hidden from the sight of the men in the house.

"But you're not calling attention to us," she said, realizing it slowly. "They know we're up here, but we won't be targets?"

Zach paused to look up at her. "Yes, I doubt Ryan will come looking. He's on a tight schedule, and I'm betting he'll move it up. When the stuff gets here tomorrow morning, he'll load everything and ship it out right away."

"Why do you think that?"

"It's what I'd do in his place." He went back to building the fire.

"And you'll follow the shipment?"

"Yes." He didn't look up.

"Even though Ryan *knows* you'll follow him?"

"Yes."

Teddy bit her lip, staring at him. She felt suddenly cold and a little lonely. He was behind his armor, out of reach. Safer for him—but hell for her. *Already*, she thought. *Already he's putting me out of his life.*

"We're safe up here?" She heard her own voice, as if from a great distance, and she stood up.

"Safe enough."

Ignoring the throb of protest from her arm, Teddy caught the hem of her sweater and peeled it off over her head, tossing it aside. Her boots landed beside the sweater, and she tugged the tail of her shirt from inside her jeans. When Zach rose and turned, she was unbuttoning the shirt.

He didn't move for a moment, and even in the dimness of the cave she could see his face tighten. "Teddy—"

She didn't take her eyes off him, and her voice was husky when she spoke. "Hell . . . call it lust."

He made a rough sound and took two steps, catching her shoulders in his large hands. "Don't, honey."

"Why not?" Teddy wondered what was in her face to make his change so; he looked as if he were in pain. "You're going to send me away, aren't you? If not tomorrow, then later." The shirt hung open, and she fumbled with the snap of her jeans. "Why shouldn't I take what I can get now? And I'm greedy, Zach; I want everything I can get from you—"

"Don't." He was holding her face, turning it up,

kissing her with aching tenderness. His eyes were glittering pools of darkness, and a muscle flexed in his jaw. "Just don't. I won't let you talk like that."

"Then shut me up," she whispered, rising on her toes as her arms slid around his neck.

The small fire crackling just a few feet away had not even begun to warm the cavelet, but neither of them noticed the chill. Their clothing fell away, dropping unnoticed to the hard dirt beneath their feet. Teddy had forgotten her injury and made him forget it, moving sensuously against him, frantic to transport them both to the only place he'd allow them to be together, to drive him so crazy that he'd forget all about sending her out of his life.

Gritting her teeth against the hot, untamed passion that fought to control her body, Teddy kept just enough command over herself to concentrate totally on pleasing him. She explored his big body with trembling fingers and shaking lips, elated by the fiery response she could feel in him. And she felt a giddy sense of power when he leashed his own powerful strength, rolling onto his back to let her do as she wished.

And what she wished was to please him, because in doing that she was pleasing herself. The wildness of what she felt added instinct to knowledge, and she was utterly uninhibited in loving him, until finally it was she who held him down, she whose fierce determination and hungry caresses stole from him every last shred of conscious will and made him helpless in the only way a very strong man could be made helpless—powerless to control or fight the need she had ignited in him.

Zach groaned harshly and lifted her bodily above him, his hard hands guiding her hips until they were fully joined. Teddy gazed down at him, her eyes shimmering with amber fire. She set the tempo, enjoying his body while hers held him tightly in a velvet clasp. With lithe muscles and a sensuous grace, she moved in a slow, lazy dance of seduction until finally he couldn't take any more.

He took over, guiding her hips, his body surging beneath her. With a strength she could never match, he drove them both higher and higher, until Teddy collapsed on him with a wild moan, even as a raw cry of release was torn from his throat.

The heat of their bodies insulated them from the chill of the cavelet, and the flickering firelight played over them both as darkness fell outside. At last Teddy lifted her head from his heaving chest, barely able to breathe herself.

"See what you'll be throwing away if you make me leave?" she whispered unsteadily.

He brushed a strand of red hair from her damp face, and his own face was strained, as if he were fighting himself. "Do you realize," he murmured, "that someone could have come in here and cut both our throats a few minutes ago? And that I wouldn't have heard—or cared?"

"You said we were safe."

"Safe enough, considering we're in a war."

Her chin became stubbornly firm as she heard what he was telling her. In a voice that hardly repressed anger, she told him, "I hate that woman for what she did to you."

"Teddy . . ."

"I love you, Zach. Why won't you believe that?"

"Because I can't." His voice was harsh, but his hands were gentle when he lifted her off him.

"Zach—"

Leaving her, he reached for his clothes and began dressing. "We're good in bed together, Teddy, and that's all." He was struggling to lock his own feelings away inside him, cold with the knowledge that they could have been in danger and he wouldn't have been able to react fast enough. This had to stop; it had to stop *now*. "For God's sake, let it be!"

"No!" She rose on her knees, glaring up at him. "Maybe you can't love me back, but I'll be damned if I'll let you send me away knowing you don't believe I love you. Do you think I'm stupid? Do you think I don't know the difference between love and—and propinquity?"

Zach gathered her clothes and tossed them to her without looking at her. His face was hard again. He had to close her out. He couldn't protect her while she was so close. His chest was aching again. "Propinquity? Well, I guess that's as good a word as any. You're just confused, Teddy. Anybody would be."

"Confused?" She made the word sound like a curse. "Confusion doesn't tear me up inside, Zach! Confusion doesn't make me so hungry that I know I'll never be full—"

Deliberately prosaic and unemotional, he said, "You haven't eaten since morning."

For the first time in her life, Teddy understood the expression "tearing out her hair." She wanted to tear hers out in sheer frustration. "Damn you, Zach."

He didn't respond to the tired curse. Instead, he said, "I'll fix something," and knelt to rummage in the duffel bag.

In silence Teddy dressed, and in silence she ate the packaged soup he heated over the fire. Time was running out for her, and she was all too aware of that. And all her instincts warned her that if she didn't at least convince Zach that she loved him, she'd never see him again.

But how to convince him when he was blindly convinced that what she felt was unreal?

He went outside several times during the next hours, and each time Teddy waited unquestioningly by the small fire. He had fixed a pot of coffee, and she sipped that, aware at one point of the absurdity of crying because he'd never make coffee for her again.

When he returned that time, her eyes were dry.

Sometime after midnight, Zach grew increasingly restless, going several times to the entrance to listen intently.

"What?" she asked, startled by the sound of her voice in the stillness.

Zach returned to the fire, frowning. "I could have sworn I heard a helicopter a while ago."

"Hagen moving in early?" she asked, but without much interest.

"No, I doubt that. He wouldn't risk it."

Teddy had been filling her coffee cup again and nearly dropped the pot as she suddenly remembered what she had done so many hours before. She sent Zach an oblique glance, chewing on her bottom lip worriedly. "Zach?"

"What?" Without waiting for a response, he rose again and went to the entrance to stand, listening.

Teddy opened her mouth to confess, but her heart leapt into her throat when he moved suddenly, reaching for the gun he wore. But the movement was never completed. Zach froze, his hand gripping the gun but leaving it holstered, and his nostrils flared. Then he relaxed completely and spoke in a normal voice. To someone outside.

"What the hell are you doing here?"

And from outside, a deep male voice responded, "What gave me away?"

Zach grunted, releasing his gun and moving back to the fire. "The stuff that French countess had concocted for you about five years ago. You're upwind."

"The cologne?" Joshua Long stepped into the cavelet, dressed as ruggedly as Zach but looking more like a country gentleman. His handsome face was mildly annoyed. "I'll have to do something about that," he said in a disgusted tone.

"Raven probably will when the next yearly shipment arrives," Zach told him.

Josh didn't seem disturbed by the prospect. "True."

"I set snares," Zach said.

Josh nodded. "I almost fell into one of them. Almost." He followed Zach's example in hunkering down by the fire, and his cool blue eyes warmed when they found Teddy. "Hello, Teddy. It's been a long time."

She avoided Zach's sudden stare. "Josh. Yes, two years or so ago, wasn't it? That business party Daddy gave while you were in San Francisco?"

"I remember it well." He stretched his hands out to the fire, and the gold of his wedding band caught the light and gleamed brightly. He shook his head slightly. "You had a leopard on a leash, and it was as tame as a kitten around you."

"Uh-huh." Teddy cleared her throat, wondering a bit wildly when the small talk would be over and they would get down to the business of Zach strangling her.

Despite his offhand attitude, Josh was gazing beneath his lashes at each of them thoughtfully, fully aware of the tension between them. He had weighed too many executives across too many boardroom tables over the years to fail now in reading these two guarded, wary people. Still casual, he told the other man, "I found your Jeep and parked there. Lucas is watching the house, and Rafferty has a chopper standing by. Raven went to find Kelsey."

In a voice totally devoid of emotion Zach said, "I gather you two know each other?"

It was Josh who answered. "We've met a few times. Her father's Justin Tyler. You've met him yourself."

Zach remembered the tall, silver-haired industrialist who had joined Josh in a few business ventures several years back. And it was sheer chance Zach hadn't been at the party Josh had mentioned; he often attended those business affairs. So Teddy was the fascinating girl with the leopard on a leash Josh had told him about. What would have happened, Zach wondered, if they had met then, under normal circumstances? He forced himself to listen as Josh went on calmly.

"We'd found out you were here in Colorado, of course, but we wouldn't have known where to look if Teddy hadn't gotten in touch this morning."

"You didn't tell me you knew anything about computers," Zach said mildly to Teddy.

She was hugging her raised knees, her chin resting on them as she gazed steadfastly into the fire. "You didn't ask."

"The access codes?"

She managed a shrug. "I paid attention when you called."

Zach drew a deep breath and let it out slowly. Ignoring her, he looked at Josh. "You can help me by getting out of here, Josh. And by taking her with you."

Teddy stiffened but still refused to look at him.

She wished she could hate him. Hate couldn't hurt worse than this, it *couldn't*.

Josh drew out a gold cigarette case and didn't reply until his cigarette was lighted. Then, completely calm, he said, "I seem to recall a few occasions when you tagged along against my wishes to make certain I didn't shoot myself, Zach. We're staying."

"Dammit, it's Clay Ryan."

Josh's blue eyes flickered and his lean face hardened, but his voice remained undisturbed when he spoke. "Yeah, I know. Lucas found that out. All the more reason."

"Josh—"

"We all know what's involved," Josh told him. "When the shipment goes out, we can take turns following so they'll never know they're being tailed."

Zach looked at Teddy again. "You certainly didn't leave anything out," he said coldly.

With equal coldness she said, "I believe in detail."

Zach rose with an almost uncontrolled motion. "I'll go talk to Lucas."

"You won't convince him, either," Josh murmured.

Zach said something violently explicit that would have had most employers' hair standing on end, and stalked from the cavelet.

Josh flicked a bit of ash from his cigarette into the fire and said musingly, "He's more than usually touchy. I haven't seen him like this in years."

Teddy didn't ask when. Instead, she said, "He told me he didn't have a kind bone in his body."

After a moment Josh said thoughtfully, "Well, actually, he doesn't."

"I thought you were his friend."

Josh looked at her, and his hard, handsome face

softened in an expression of gentleness that few ever saw. In a tone to match his expression he said, "Teddy, people do brutal things to each other, and Zach's spent too many years watching that. He's been through a hellish war and a great many battles. He's a strong man, and strong men don't fall apart when they're hurt. They just keep getting tougher. He isn't kind. He's the best man I know, but he isn't kind."

Staring at him, Teddy slowly began to understand. "But . . . if he does something that's kind?"

"Then he has his reasons, and they'll be personal and deeply felt—not abstract. He hates gunrunners because he's seen what guns do in the wrong hands. He hates criminals because he's seen what *they* do. He isn't afraid of anything that breathes. And there's nothing he won't do for a friend."

She returned her gaze to the fire. "I love him," she said suddenly, without thinking.

"I thought so," Josh said quietly.

Josh met Zach outside when he heard the whistled signal that he knew was meant to draw him out. "Any luck?" he asked dryly.

"No, and you damn well know it. Josh, you won't leave?"

"Sorry." He didn't sound it.

Zach sighed, accepting what he couldn't change. "Dammit, my job is supposed to be to protect you."

"You're on vacation," Josh reminded him politely.

Acknowledging the hit with a grunt, Zach said, "All right, then. If you won't leave, then you won't. Look, I'm going to take Teddy to the Jeep at first light, and she'll stay put there until we all move out."

"Will she?"

"If I have to tie and gag her," Zach said grimly, "she'll stay there. She caught a graze from Ryan's gun this morning, charging where she shouldn't have in a misguided attempt to save my hide. I won't let it happen again."

Josh studied his friend as well as he could in the darkness, remarking only, "You know best, I'm sure."

If there was any sarcasm intended, Zach didn't hear it. "I'll see you in the morning, then."

"Right." Josh started away from the cavelet, then looked over his shoulder to say softly, "Zach? Justin happened to mention to me once that Teddy's an expert marksman." He didn't wait to see the effect of his words but disappeared silently into the darkness.

Entering the cavelet, Zach said accusingly, "You didn't tell me you could handle guns."

"You didn't ask." She was sitting as he'd left her, but subdued now rather than stiff. And when she looked up at him with those huge doe eyes of hers, Zach had trouble remaining angry. He tried, though. "Why'd you call out the troops?"

Returning her gaze to the fire, Teddy murmured, "Because you aren't bulletproof, armor or no armor."

"What?"

"I was worried about you, Zach. And I rather like your body without a lot of bullets in it."

"I could have handled it, Teddy."

"I know." She sighed. "But I couldn't."

After a moment, because there wasn't anything else to say, Zach told her to turn in and get some sleep. Tomorrow would be busy. And Teddy crawled into the sleeping bag without a word, unsurprised when he remained by the fire, watchful and alert.

Sometime later, unable to sleep, Teddy asked a quiet question.

"Zach, what's the law of the jungle?"

He answered almost automatically, "Travel light, fast, and alone." Then he looked at her, frowning a little. "Why?"

"No reason."

Neither of them said anything more, but after he'd turned back to the fire, a verse from Kipling flitted through Teddy's head. And she denied it silently, fiercely. Just because Zach had broken a part of that law . . . just because *she* was hung around his neck like a millstone and his friends were here . . .

Damn Kipling.

It wasn't Zach's fault that events had conspired to shake him off his normal balance. No matter how reckless he sometimes seemed, he was always cautious, shrewd, and methodical and was rarely caught off guard.

But for Zack, the past days had been trying, to say the least. What should have remained simply a job of surveillance at least until the last minute had turned into a deadly game of cat and mouse. He should have had only his own hide to worry about, instead of first one other, and then several others. And during a situation when emotional distractions were hardly something he could afford, he never should have been forced to deal with Teddy's emotions and his own.

Still, Zach had a broad back, and he could carry these burdens. It was the final one that broke him.

With everything else, he never should have had to crawl inside the twisted mind of a criminal and think as that other man thought, plan as that other man did.

He never should have had to search that other mind for weaknesses, even as his own were being shrewdly pondered. But he had to. And he tried. And it wasn't his fault that his mind was filled with too many diverse problems and couldn't quite handle one more.

So nobody blamed him for what happened. Except Zach.

Zach blamed himself.

He woke Teddy at dawn, and she ate the soup he had prepared in silence. She didn't object when he told her where he was taking her, and followed him silently through the woods without protest or noise of any kind. When they reached the Jeep, Zach put her inside and gave her the keys.

Zach hesitated before closing the door, looking at her small, vital face and big, doelike eyes. Then, because he couldn't help himself, he leaned into the vehicle and kissed her, deeply and thoroughly. A lover's kiss. When he finally drew back, her eyes seemed brighter than before.

"I'm sorry I called them, Zach," she whispered.

His fingers lingered on her cheek for a moment, and then Zach straightened and closed the door. "Stay put. I'll be back."

"All right."

By the time Zach reached the house again, the sun was up. He made his way cautiously through the thick growth until he encountered Josh and

Lucas, neither of whom looked much the worse for wear after a night without sleep. All three men were unshaven, wore rugged clothing, and held guns. They looked more like hunters one would expect to find in the area.

"Anything?" Zach asked, crouching beside them.

Josh shook his head. "Nothing. Lucas is circling the house every fifteen minutes or so. So far there's been no movement. When's the shipment expected?"

"Any time."

They waited in silence. A few minutes later Lucas melted away into the woods, leaving Josh and Zach alone.

"Teddy's at the Jeep?" Josh asked then.

"Yes."

Josh sent him a glance before returning his attention to the house. After a moment he said quietly, "She did what she had to do, Zach."

"I know."

"She loves you."

Zach's jaw tightened. "She thinks she does."

"Oh, is that how it is?" Since their friendship had never precluded honesty, sometimes voiced harshly, Josh made no attempt to soften his sardonic tone. "Just her imagination, I suppose? And what about you, Zach? Are you *imagining* whatever it is that's ripping at your guts right now?"

"Drop it, Josh."

"The hell I will. It wasn't so long ago that you made me face up to some possibilities about Raven. It's my turn now. Are you going to be fool enough to let that girl go? Can you possibly be that pigheaded?"

"Josh—"

He was interrupted curtly. "If you can't see that Teddy's vastly different from that spoiled debutante you brought out of the jungle, then you need your thick head examined. Badly."

What Zach might have replied—and explosively, too—was never voiced, because Lucas returned somewhat breathlessly to their side just then. "I think we've got trouble," he told them grimly.

"What kind?" Zach asked.

"I crossed the tracks you made coming back from the Jeep, Zach. There was another set almost on top of them—heading for the house. Tracks of a large man, but too deep for the size. As if he were carrying something heavy."

"Carrying—" Zach realized in one awful, crashing second what had happened, and the tightness in his chest was squeezing the breath out of him. He had made one simple miscalculation, one tiny, dreadful mistake. He had forgotten that Ryan knew of Teddy's presence, forgotten that an innocent victim was quite often the best tool, the most deadly weapon a vicious man could use.

Ryan had crawled into *his* head.

Ryan meant to go on with his plan, all right. He intended to load up his shipment and send it out under Zach's nose. And he had waited patiently in order to get himself some gilt-edged insurance just to make certain that Zach could only watch helplessly.

"Zach?" Josh was gripping his arm, but Zach barely felt those powerful fingers. "Zach, dammit, don't go off the deep end!"

Utterly still and unnaturally calm, Zach looked at him. "I'm fine," he said mildly.

Josh didn't let go; he knew his friend was a long way from being fine. He knew what the deadly pallor and blank eyes meant. And he wished hopelessly that Clay Ryan could also know, because then he would not use Teddy as hostage for Zach's good behavior. Not even a madman would try using her.

A voice called out suddenly from the house, vicious and ringing with triumph.

"Steele? You out there, Steele?"

Vaguely, Zach decided that it was good Ryan knew his name. A man should always know the name of his executioner.

"Steele? I've got your redhead. You stay out of my way and I might give her back to you. But if you don't back off right now, I'll start sending out pieces of her, and you can listen to her scream. Got that, Steele? I hope you have. She's a cute little thing. I'd hate to have to hurt her."

And then Teddy screamed.

Seven

Teddy never saw it coming. She was daydreaming, remembering that last fleeting moment of tenderness in Zach's eyes and hoping against hope that everything would be all right. Feeling safe, she had rolled the Jeep's window down, and so had deprived herself of even the instant's warning of an opening door. One moment she was breathing in the chill morning air, and the next a white cloth smelling sickly sweet was clamped over her nose and mouth.

After that she was conscious only of blackness for a while. Gradually, though, she felt movement, and heard muted voices. The movement stopped and there was quiet. She was lying on something soft—a bed, perhaps. Her hands were tied behind her back. There was something familiar, she thought, in that.

Ah, yes. The big man with the dangerous face and soft voice had tied her to a tree and then drowned her car. She remembered. He'd carried her over his shoulder; that was why her ribs ached. And any minute now he'd untie her wrists and find a salve for the bruises. Any minute now he'd pour her coffee and make the instinctive fear go away and . . . and kiss her, make love to her until she couldn't think and—

No. No, that had already happened. Why was it happening again?

Teddy's eyes snapped open to the strangeness of a room and an unfamiliar face watching her. She caught her breath on a gasp, coldness sweeping over her.

"I'm glad you're awake," the man smiling down at her as if everything were normal said.

He was a tall man, broad across the shoulders and powerful. His face was regular of feature, his eyes empty of color or expression, his smile filled with even, white teeth and impersonal ferocity. He was leaning negligently against a tall corner post of the bed she lay in, appearing unthreatening and almost lazy.

Teddy had never been so afraid of a man in her life.

In a conversational tone he told her, "It's a pity you got involved in this. Your lover means to interfere in my work, and I can't allow that. You understand, don't you? It's purely business. I must have those guns. Oh, he told you, didn't he, about the guns? Certainly he did."

Clay Ryan studied her appraisingly. "You're his Achilles' heel. Lucky that I discovered that."

Keep him talking! Teddy thought. "How did you—"

"How did I discover that? You forget, sweetheart. I was the one aiming the gun yesterday morning when you took the bullet meant for him. Odd, isn't it, that you and I were the ones wounded, while he remains unscathed?"

For the first time Teddy noticed the bulge of a bandage under his shirt. On his left arm. Just like her.

Ryan was smiling his empty white smile, and his eyes roved over her body with an enjoyment that sickened her. "Pity we don't have more time," he murmured.

Teddy stiffened when he bent down suddenly, but he only grasped her uninjured arm and pulled her up off the bed. Everything about him repelled her, particularly the heat of his body when he stood behind her at an open window.

She barely listened as he shouted his message to Zach, trying desperately to think of some way out of this. It was then she became conscious of the heavy weight of her purse against her hip; she had slung the strap across her chest, bandolier fashion, before leaving the cave with Zach.

The weight of it told her that Ryan hadn't bothered to search the purse, and so hadn't found her dart pistol. It was a piece of luck she hadn't counted on.

But with her hands tied behind her back, there wasn't a chance she could get to the pistol and use it, even if he left her alone to try. The penknife . . . maybe if she could get to that . . . but with her hands tied—

There was nothing she could do, and her only comfort was the knowledge that at least two other men waited outside the house with Zach. They'd keep him from being reckless, she thought. They *would*.

Even with some knowledge of the kind of man Ryan was, Teddy wasn't prepared for what happened then. She hadn't realized that Ryan had crawled into Zach's head quite so thoroughly and that he had a shrewd idea of just what was needed to paralyze his enemy at least temporarily. Not just the knowledge that Zach's woman was being held as hostage but that Ryan would hurt that woman without compunction.

Teddy wasn't braced for the blow, and when Ryan's big fist struck her wounded arm and sent pain knifing all the way to the top of her skull, her scream was pure reflex.

When the drawn-out cry of agony reached the three men outside, it wasn't at all clear to Josh and Lucas that they could hold back their friend. Only Josh's quick, urgent reminder to Zach of the danger to Teddy of storming the house kept the big man still. And even then, the muscles of his powerful frame bunched and rippled in a blind response to his rage and his fear for her.

"We have an edge," Josh was saying firmly. "He thinks you're out here alone, and one man can attack from only one direction. We'll get her out, Zach."

They were all distracted then—even Zach—by the rumbling of a big truck pulling into the drive from the main road.

To Lucas, Josh said, "Call Rafferty. Have him get airborne and follow the truck when it leaves here. Cautiously."

"Right." Lucas melted into the trees, heading for the vehicle he'd hidden off the road.

Josh returned his attention to Zach, speaking in the most even voice he could manage and concentrating all his powerful will on the determined effort to hold his friend just this side of sanity as long as possible.

He didn't think he could manage it for long with Teddy in danger.

"Ryan would have disabled your Jeep and my car, too—which, if we're lucky, he'll believe is Teddy's. Lucas has a van, so we've a way out of here once we get Teddy. He's holding her as a threat to keep you from interfering, but he isn't likely to take her with him. He'll want the truck to get a head start, and he can't mean to be far behind himself. Think, Zach. Is there anything in that house he could use to keep us here and make it impossible for us to get to Teddy even after he leaves?"

Zach was staring toward the house, watching as three men busily moved between the house and truck carrying bundles and boxes. After a moment he spoke in a flat, mild tone. "Explosives. And he knows how to use them."

"So do we," Josh reminded him matter-of-factly. "You've defused more than one bomb, and so have I. And you did enough background on Ryan to have found a pattern if there is one. Is there? I know he uses a different method with every job, but how about with explosives? He's used them before, more than once. Does he favor any one type?"

It didn't appear as though Zach were listening, but he responded to the question in the same level, docile tone. "Plastic explosives. Enough to bring the house down. Timed-fuse or remote-control detonator."

Josh looked at him worriedly. "All right, then we know what we'll have to deal with. We can handle it, Zach. We'll get her out safely."

"Yes," Zach said.

• • •

The pain in her arm had settled to a dully throbbing ache, but Teddy was unable to think clearly again until she found herself tied securely to the bed. She heard voices from downstairs, the rumble of a truck pulling up at the front door, and looked up at Ryan as he tied her wrists tightly to the headboard. She wondered vaguely when he had untied them behind her back and then retied them, disgusted with herself for a missed opportunity even though she probably couldn't have taken advantage of it.

Ryan was strong.

"You don't know what you've done," she whispered, only half aware of speaking at all.

He laughed curtly. "I've quite effectively hamstrung your lover, sweetheart. He won't dare rush the house or interfere in any way with my plans. His Jeep is disabled and so is your car, and the communications equipment he has is useless to him." Ryan gagged her securely with a strip of white cloth, then patted her cheek consolingly.

"But don't worry. Steele will hike to the nearest phone and call an army up here, so you won't have to wait too long all by your lonesome. You'll certainly be his first priority, and I'll be getting my stuff out of here while he worries about you. Bye, sweetheart."

Teddy stared at the door as it closed behind him. The gag prevented her from making a sound, but her thoughts were clear.

Fool. He *is* an army.

It took half an hour for the big semi to be loaded,

and the watchers counted all three of Ryan's men and the driver in the truck when it pulled out again.

The house looked deserted, only the single car Ryan and his henchmen had used remaining in the drive.

Without a word Zach had left to go back up to the cavelet, and Josh made no effort to stop him. Lucas, who had just returned from making a cautious circuit around the house, got back in time to see the big man disappear into the woods.

"Where's he going?"

"To get his tools."

"Which tools?" Lucas asked warily.

"The ones he designed for precision work. You want to bet Ryan hasn't got the house wired?"

"Not really, no." Lucas sighed. "Boss, I think he's gone already. Ryan. I couldn't find any fresh tracks, and there's no sign of another car, but I think he got out somehow. It just *feels* like he's gone."

Musing, Josh said, "He wouldn't have given Zach a final warning. Wouldn't have threatened to blow the house up with Teddy in it if Zach came too close."

"He wants Zach dead," Lucas agreed. "He'd expect him to go in after Teddy sooner or later."

"Ummm. And he wouldn't have wanted to travel with that stolen artwork—but *would* have wanted to keep a close eye on it. Call Rafferty again."

"Find out if there's somebody following the truck? Gotcha." He hesitated on the point of leaving. "Boss? I've only seen Zach this way once before, and you stopped him then. D'you think— ?"

"No. Not this time." Unemotionally, Josh said, "Clay Ryan's a dead man."

Lucas opened his mouth to speak, apparently thought better of it, and went to call Rafferty.

Out of an automatic sense of caution Josh tested the direction of the wind before lighting a cigarette. He stubbed it out a few moments later when Zach appeared silently at his side. "Lucas thinks Ryan's flown the coop," he advised tersely.

"He has good instincts." Zach's opaque gaze flickered toward the house and the hand holding a large leather pouch tightened until the knuckles shone white. "Teddy . . ."

In the same bracing tone Josh said, "Inside is our bet. She's bait, Zach, to get you in there."

Calmly, Zach said, "It's working."

To Josh, that was unnecessary information. "He hasn't had time to rig up anything fancy, Zach. I mean, he may well have the house wired top to bottom, but he hasn't had time to—to booby-trap a hostage."

Still utterly calm, Zach said, "So getting in without setting off a bomb will be the trick." He rose abruptly. "I have to go now."

"Zach—"

Beneath the layers of icy cold, Zach's mind was working methodically. "If I were him," he mused softly, "I would have rigged no more than a fifteen-minute fuse. Time enough to realize he had gone. Time enough to get inside the house. There'll be a secondary bomb rigged and hidden. Not time enough to find and defuse that. And not time enough for me to find Teddy and get her out."

Rising, Josh said urgently, "Wait. Just a minute. We need to know if he'd really gone."

"I can't—"

"Zach, he could be standing by somewhere with a remote, ready to blow the house as soon as you get inside. We have to know he can't see what we're doing."

Lucas reached them then, a little breathless. "Bingo," he said, panting. "I think. Rafferty says there's a nice, unassuming sedan following the semi."

That was all Zach needed. "You two stay here—"

"Forget it," Josh said briefly.

If Zach had been thinking of anything other than getting to Teddy, he likely would have decked both his friends and gone on alone. But in his present condition such strategy was a bit beyond him. Besides, he needed help to get her out and defuse the bomb, because no man could be in two places at the same time. So he simply headed for the house.

It took no more than five minutes alone for Teddy to feel an abrupt, bloody-minded temper rising. She was on her back, bound head and foot, gagged, helpless. She hated being helpless. It was one thing, she realized, to take comfort in the protection of a strong man and quite another to await rescue feebly, like some delicate princess in an ivory tower.

She tilted her head back against the pillow and stared up at her wrists. The knot looked all too secure, dammit. But the rope was fastened to a decorative metal ring in the headboard, and maybe, just maybe . . . Carefully, she jerked her bound wrists away from the headboard. They moved only a few inches, and her left arm protested in a jolt of agony that took her breath.

Teddy rubbed her cheek against the aching arm. She felt wetness and thought she was crying, but then realized that Ryan's rough teatment, and her own, had broken the wound open again. She was bleeding.

Maybe not much time, then.

She locked her teeth down on the gag, held on to what she could of the rope to spare her wrists, and jerked again. And again.

By the third jerk, the wetness on her face was indeed tears, and she was breathing in sobbing gasps. But she kept jerking, fighting waves of pain and nausea, struggling to remain conscious. And finally, the metal ring tore loose, and her bound wrists fell heavily to her stomach. Through the hot tears filling her eyes she could see that the left sleeve of her dark sweater was stained with blood. Not much blood, though; she could at least be thankful for that.

Teddy counted slowly to twenty before she could find the strength to sit up, then closed her eyes at the wave of dizziness. Her jaw was aching, and she realized that her teeth were still gritted. She relaxed her jaw, and her breathing gradually steadied.

Even though she'd tried to protect them, the rope hadn't been kind to her wrists; there was a little blood, a great deal of chafing, and her hands had swelled a bit from loss of circulation. She flexed the stiff fingers, wincing as the blood returned to them, and then fumbled to draw her purse around so that she could open it. Not for the first time, she cursed her pack-rat habits as she scrabbled through the jumble in search of the small penknife. Finding it at last, she sawed through the rope between her wrists, sacrificing a bit more skin in the process. The pain barely disturbed her; she was very conscious of the passing minutes and far too aware of several much more disturbing facts.

She had seen Ryan's face, and he didn't leave witnesses.

He had left her alone far too long; there was something wrong with that.

He hated Zach, hated him and wanted him dead.

And something else, there was something—

Explosives.

Ryan had nearly killed Zach once with explosives. Would he try a second time? Set a trap with her as bait—

"You're his Achilles' heel."

Teddy tore off the gag and went to work on her bound ankles. She wanted to call out, to scream a warning to Zach, but didn't dare. She had heard the big truck leave mintues before, but what if Ryan was still nearby? With a remote detonator in one hand and a meaningless white smile on his face, waiting for Zach to get inside the house—and Zach would get inside, would come after her.

She scrambled off the bed and dug in her purse for the tranquilizer gun. It wasn't much, but it was all she had.

The door swung open.

Teddy whirled, leveling the gun automatically in a two-handed grip, knowing she might have only one chance. And the blond man in the doorway took a hasty step back, his own gun pointing quickly at the ceiling.

"Whoa! I'm with Zach!"

She stared at him for a moment, then said, "Lucas Kendrick?"

"Right." He didn't ask how she recognized him but turned his head to call loudly, "I've found her. She's fine."

Teddy straightened and returned her dart pistol to her purse. "Where's Zach? Ryan might have a bomb."

"He left two. Zach's defusing the second one now. If he can't do it, we've got five minutes before it blows." Lucas's sharp blue eyes narrowed. "Is that blood on your cheek?"

"From my arm. It started bleeding again." She lifted a hand to wipe away the smear of blood, and Lucas swore softly. He returned his gun to its shoulder holster and produced a snowy handkerchief from his pocket.

He was tearing the square of linen in two as he moved to stand before her and, obviously seeing her anxious impatience, explained quickly as he began to wrap one of her wrists. "If Zach sees blood on you, he's likely to go right around the bend and do something really crazy. Did that bastard do this?"

Suddenly aware that she could no longer even move her left arm, Teddy concentrated all her will on just remaining on her feet and coherent. "No, I did that getting loose."

"Must hurt like hell," he commented with sympathy.

"I can't feel anything," she responded honestly. "Can't move my arm, either."

"Josh said you were wounded yesterday."

"Ummm. Ryan hit my arm. That's why I screamed."

Lucas's handsome face went decidedly grim, but he said nothing. He wrapped her wrists as carefully as possible, noting quickly that the blood on her sweater was obvious, but only close-up. She was very pale, but clearly determined to remain on her feet. He admired both her courage and her obvious strength.

She'd done a damn good job of getting herself out

of this mess, and he wouldn't soon forget the resolution in her small face as she'd expertly aimed that gun at him. He wondered if Zach knew what a tough lady she really was.

He gently tugged the sleeves of her sweater down to hide the makeshift bandages, then said, "Let's go."

Teddy was grateful that he kept a light but firm hold on her right arm as he led her from the room. She wasn't at all sure she could have made it on her own.

The house was a large one, the bedrooms they passed sparsely furnished, most of them with covers over everything. A curving staircase led down into an open foyer, and Josh Long was waiting for them at the bottom.

Teddy was dimly aware that some silent signal passed between the two men, but she had no time to react before Lucas had hurried away and Josh swung her easily up into his arms.

He carried her toward the front door.

"Wait! Where's Zach?"

"He'll be along. Dammit, Teddy, be still!"

She dug into reserves of strength she hadn't known she had and struggled harder to escape him, staring back over his shoulder as he carried her from the house. "No! Put me down! I want to go to Zach—"

"It'd be more than my life's worth to let you go back in that house," he told her grimly. "Teddy, he'll be fine. If he can't defuse the bomb with a minute left, Lucas'll pull him out of there."

Wildly, she said, "Pull him out? He won't be able to pull him out! He's a damned *army*; nobody could pull him out! He'll stay till the last bloody *second* and get his stubborn, macho hide blown to bits! Josh, let me go!"

"Listen to me," Josh ordered harshly. "Now that you're safe, the single thought in Zach's mind is to get Ryan. And he is not about to let himself be blown to bits while that man is still walking around. There's nothing in that house worth dying for. He'll come out, Teddy."

That argument made sense, but rational though it was, nothing could ease the agonized fear for her man. Still, she forced herself to stop struggling, and when Josh set her on her feet at the edge of the woods, she didn't try to run back into the house. She stood perfectly still, staring toward the house, her nails biting into her palms.

"How much longer?" she asked in a husky whisper.

Josh, who had rarely taken his eyes from his watch, replied tautly, "A minute and a half."

"He has to come out." She barely recognized the queerly conversational voice as her own. "He just has to, that's all. He doesn't even know if . . . if we— He can't die not *knowing*. He won't do that. Even if it isn't likely, it's still possible, and he'd want to know. He'd want to—*Zach!*"

Josh leaned back against a sturdy tree and, in a detached manner, watched his hands shake. Then he looked up to see Zach being engulfed by a distraught redhead. Speaking to Lucas as the other man reached him, he said heavily, "I'm getting too old for this sort of thing."

"You and me both." Lucas was looking a bit white around the mouth, but his voice was steady. "A minute twenty-five left on the clock, and he never turned a hair. Is there *anything* that can shake that granite foundation of his?"

Josh glanced again toward the couple several yards away and spoke softly. "One thing. One small thing."

Teddy found that she could move her left arm, after all, at least enough to get it around Zach's neck. And she gloried in the strength of his arms as they held her tightly against him. In a fierce, shaking tone she said, "Don't you *ever* do that to me again!"

He hugged her, hard. "I'm sorry, honey. I should have known he'd go for you," Zach murmured against her neck. "It's my fault he got you."

Teddy drew back and stared at him, hardly aware that her boots dangled well above the ground. "Since when d'you read minds?" she demanded, finding that much of her strength had returned in the security of his embrace.

"I know his mind," Zach said gruffly. "I should have known what he'd do."

Teddy said something derisive, and it wasn't "malarkey."

Zach grinned in spite of himself. "You never should have learned words like that. Or at least not learned how to *use* them like that."

Peering at him owlishly almost nose-to-nose, she said. "Listen, when I was a little girl, I played jacks under my father's boardroom tables. They usually forgot I was there. I learned how to use a *lot* of words I shouldn't have learned."

He kissed her and then set her gently on her feet but kept an arm around her shoulders. "You'll have to tell me, maybe I'll learn something."

Suddenly remembering that the danger was far

from past, she said fiercely, "I'll tell you a few of them now if you're planning to do something crazy!"

"Who, me?" Zach looked up as Josh and Lucas approached, both weighted down with Teddy's bags and as much of Zach's equipment as they could carry.

Succinctly, Lucas said, "I say we get the hell out of Dodge."

"And head for Tombstone," Josh murmured. "Zach, weren't there supposed to be some federal marshals called up here? Now would be the time. I'd say there was a fair amount of physical evidence in the house."

Tombstone. OK Corral. Gun battle. Finally, the remainder of Josh's comments sank in. With a slight start Teddy exclaimed, "Ryan left fingerprints, I know that. He wasn't wearing gloves when he tied me to the bed, and he touched the headboard. I'll bet he touched the explosives too."

Zach looked down at her. "When he tied you to the bed? He tied you to a bed?"

"I didn't tell him that," Lucas murmured.

Since Zach was on her left side and that arm had gone numb again, Teddy couldn't manage a reassuring hug. But she did manage a bright—and slightly wary—smile. "He was a perfect gentleman," she said, editing the truth somewhat. "And I'm just fine, after all."

"You screamed," Zach said, his voice going placid and remote in a way she recognized.

"I was scared," Teddy retorted stoutly.

Josh and Lucas, fascinated spectators to this, looked back and forth as though at a tennis match.

"You were hurting."

Teddy, who still had hopes of getting her warrior through all this without him going berserk and spilling precious blood, like his own, wasn't about to admit that Ryan had nearly caused her to pass out with his cruel blow.

"You weren't there," she told him.

"I know pain when I hear it."

"Your imagination."

"There's blood on your sleeve."

"I did that getting loose." Hastily, she looked at the other two men. "Can we go now? Let's go."

Lucas started slightly, jolted rudely from fascination, then turned. "This way," he directed carefully, after clearing his throat.

They were all silent as they made their way through the woods to where Lucas had parked his van. Their stuff was loaded, then Zach helped Teddy into the backseat, climbed in after her, and pulled her securely onto his lap.

She didn't object.

The other two men got in front, with Lucas driving, and it wasn't until the van pulled out onto the main road that Zach spoke.

"West?"

Josh half turned to look at him, his eyes narrowing at his friend's tone. "That's the way the semi went. Why?"

"Because," Zach said heavily, "the guns are supposed to be waiting east of here. Along with Kelsey, probably Hagen, and by now, half a dozen federal marshals. That's why."

Teddy rested her head on Zach's shoulder and closed her eyes. She didn't really pay attention to the ensuing discussion but remembered it all very well later.

Josh used the van's radio to contact the helicopter

where Rafferty was to relay several messages. On a particular frequency he was to summon the marshals to the house. On another frequency he was to contact Josh's wife—who was apparently in search of someone named Kelsey—and explain where the guns were supposed to be but probably weren't. And on yet another frequency he was to try to contact Hagen, on whom all four of the men seemed somewhat determined to get their hands.

After that Teddy went to sleep.

The van rolled along in silence for a while, until Zach was certain Teddy was asleep. Then, directing his words at their driver, he said, "Now you can tell me."

Lucas glanced in the rearview mirror, then at Josh, and sighed. "When I found her, she was fine, Zach. I don't know how she'd managed to get herself loose, but she was on her feet—and ready for anything. She had a gun pointed at me and looked like she knew how to use it."

"Gun?"

"Yeah. Put it in her purse."

With less hesitation this time, Zach dug into Teddy's purse and produced the gun. He stared at it for a moment, and then his lips twitched. In a slightly unsteady voice he said solemnly, "She was loaded for bear, all right."

"That's what I thought," Lucas agreed.

Zach cleared his throat. "The four-legged kind."

After a beat Lucas said blankly, "What?" and Josh looked back over his shoulder at the gun and began smiling.

"Real bears," Zach explained. "Furry bears. I don't

know much about dosage, but I'd say this would have decked a hungry grizzly bent on getting his next meal. You certainly would have taken a nice long nap."

"Are you saying—"

"Tranquilizers, Luc. This is a dart pistol."

Lucas let out a long-suffering sigh. "Figures," he said.

She was nothing more than a shadow, dressed all in black, and made not a sound as she moved into the warehouse. But she didn't continue to lurk in the darkness; instead, she moved confidently into the dim circle of a so-called security light, folded her arms, and waited.

She didn't have to wait long.

Kelsey moved into the circle, looking more pained than surprised. "Don't tell me you trailed me here," he begged. "I know you're good, but you're also supposed to be out of touch these days."

Raven Long smiled at him, her merry violet eyes dancing. "We never gave our contacts away—even to each other, remember? And I kept mine. They got me within twenty miles of here. I'd already settled on the munitions dump as the likeliest place when I got word you were here for sure."

"Got word from whom?"

"Josh—via Rafferty. You just might be guarding the wrong rat hole, chum."

Kelsey stared at her for a moment, then said several things he must have learned in rough places. Still exercising his colorful vocabulary, he found a crowbar and pried off the lids of several crates. His language became more colorful as each crate was opened.

Raven didn't look to see what he'd found; she didn't have to. Interspersed among his more colorful phrases were listings of such things as machine parts, nuts and bolts, hubcaps and crankshafts.

In a detached tone she said, "I suppose the art collectors must have some pretty shrewd people working for them. Or else Ryan met with them and arranged it. They waited until this shipment was spotted and then somehow got in and replaced the crates with dummies."

In a tone approaching a groan Kelsey said, "And the boss pulled back the marshals when he found out your gang was coming in on this. He said there'd be too many watchers for the job. Great. That's just great."

"Where are the marshals?" she asked briskly.

Kelsey got a grip on himself. "An hour or so away. With Hagen."

"You can reach them?"

"Sure."

"Then you'd better. Rafferty's in a helicopter following the semi, and what is presumably Ryan's car. Josh, Lucas, Zach, and a lady named Teddy are in a van somewhere behind. Everybody's heading west."

For a moment Kelsey allowed himself to be unwillingly fascinated. "A damned convoy, for crying out loud."

Politely, Raven said, "Would you mind very much getting a move on, old pal? I'd like to be with my husband before we have to circle the wagons."

"I hope you have wings."

"Next best thing. I have a foreign job with a lot of horses under the hood."

Kelsey winced. "Can I drive?"

"No."

"I was afraid you'd say that."

Raven followed him from the warehouse. Bracingly, but with a hint of laughter in her tone, she said, "Be brave, Tonto. I can hold horses on a curve."

"Uh-huh. That's what you said the *last* time."

Eight

Teddy crawled up beside Zach despite his gesture to stay back, and peered over the top of the hill where they all lay prone. Ignoring her various aches and pains, she said in a low voice, "Now what?"

In an idle tone Josh said, "Anybody got an Uzi?"

"I thought those were illegal," Teddy commented.

"This whole damn thing's illegal," Lucas reminded her.

"Oh. Right."

Zach looked at the three glum faces ranged beside him and said dryly, "There's only five of them."

"*They* have Uzis," Josh remarked.

"Then," Zach said calmly, "we'll just have to be better shots."

Teddy winced. "I don't like any of this. Those are real automatic guns down there, held by men whose faces indicate the seriousness of their states of mind. Now, I may well be an amateur at this kind of stuff, but I'd say the odds are that those guys will hit at least half of what they shoot at."

Apparently approving of her logic, Lucas said, "Why don't we just shoot each other and save them the trouble?"

"Defeatists," Zach grumbled.

Josh was smiling a little. "Okay, gang, now that we've got that out of our systems, what do we do?" And he looked at Zach, since this was, technically, his show.

Zach thoughtfully eyed the setup below. The semi holding the stolen artwork had pulled well off a little-traveled secondary road and into a fairly large clearing ringed by trees. Ryan's car had pulled in close behind, and now both were parked. Ryan's three henchmen, the semi driver, and himself were grouped between the vehicles. And even at this distance Ryan didn't seem happy.

"He didn't hear an explosion," Josh murmured.

"Would he expect to?" Lucas asked. "He got nearly a quarter of an hour's head start and had put most of a mountain between himself and the house by the time it should have blown."

"The helicopter, maybe?" Teddy guessed.

Zach nodded slowly. "Maybe. Maybe either or both. If he heard the helicopter somewhere along the way, he could be getting jumpy. Or it could be that he expected the guns to be here."

"Hello, all," a low voice murmured behind them.

Zach glanced over his shoulder, then looked at Josh somewhat balefully. "I ought to take up knitting," he said in disgust.

"They're pros at this sort of thing," Josh pointed out, amused. "We're just talented amateurs."

"Still—"

"I know. Lucas?"

"I'll keep watch. You guys caucus and decide what to do."

Josh looked at Zach, brow raised. "Caucus?"

"Getting fancy, isn't he?"

"Go to hell," Lucas muttered, struggling with a grin.

Teddy looked at them all bemusedly but followed when Zach and Josh slid back down the hill.

Waiting at the bottom were Raven Long and Kelsey, both of whom were responsible for Zach's disgust, since they'd approached without any sound or warning.

Raven, a tall, striking brunette with laughing eyes, responded to her husband's embrace with enthusiasm and said cheerfully, "Trouble. I knew you were trouble from the moment we met."

"Look who's talking." Josh kissed her, then, after a glance aside, said curiously, "What's wrong with Kelsey?"

Looking a bit queasy, Kelsey said, "Her driving, that's what's wrong with me."

Josh held his wife's shoulders and stared at her in horror. "You drove in these mountains?"

Raven patted his cheek consolingly. "Not over eighty, darling, I promise."

"Eighty-five," Kelsey said in a failing voice.

Teddy, sitting on a rock with one elbow on her knee and her chin cupped in a palm, stared at them, fascinated. There was just something about these people. A murderous gang of cutthroats over the hill, and this little group . . . Teddy had a strong feeling that these friends of Zach's were something quite out of the ordinary.

And it wasn't just that they were obviously strong people. Or even that they were courageous in an age when that was hardly a common trait. They all seemed to share another trait aside from strength and courage, something almost quixotic. It was as if, out of their varied pasts and experiences, each had emerged with a strong idealism and a secure inner vitality to cope with whatever came along. And *enjoyed* coping.

Teddy, with her sure knowledge of Zach's past and the parts these people played in it, thought that they should have lived during an age when men fought dragons. They would have been awfully good at it. She looked at Raven Long, silently deciding that the violet-eyed woman would have fought alongside her husband. And what's more, that he wouldn't have found that surprising or unusual.

Fascinating.

Raven blithely promised her husband that somebody else could drive the Porsche back to the rental company, then turned and introduced herself and Kelsey to Teddy. Responding suitably, Teddy wondered if the other woman was even conscious of the .45 automatic that was stuck inside her belt at the small of her back. She didn't seem to be.

They were all armed. Even Teddy was. . . . She thought about that. Thought about the difference between her gun and their weapons. Absently, still thinking, she followed the conversations going on around her.

"What happened to the guns?" Zach was asking Kelsey.

The other man, who had an unremarkable but curiously pleasant face and a deep voice, sounded as disgusted as Zach had earlier. "Damned if I know. They were there—and then they weren't. But I'd bet the price tag on the stolen art that the guns weren't moved while I was watching."

"Who spotted them?"

Kelsey grimaced. "A ranger, of all people. Just a routine check of the old dump. A marshal verified the guns were there, and that it was the shipment we were busy tracing on the other end. I was up here within two days, and the warehouse was *supposed* to be under guard until I got here."

They were all kneeling or sitting on the ground now, and Raven, who kneeled beside Josh with her fingers laced together over his shoulder and her chin resting on them, asked, "Just how sure are we that the trade hasn't already been made?"

Zach frowned. "You mean that the semi down there has the guns rather than the artwork?"

They were all business now, and Teddy paid attention.

"Why not?" Raven asked. "These mountain roads are hidden from the air by trees in places, and we passed through one tunnel. If an identical semi holding the guns had been waiting inside . . ."

"Ryan could be waiting for an airlift out of here," Josh suggested. "All he needed was a glance to verify the guns; they could have pulled it off in the tunnel. Rafferty had to stay back so far, he could have missed it. The other truck could have pulled off onto one of those side roads, and we'd never have seen it, even if we'd been looking for it."

Kelsey, reclining with his back against a tree, said glumly, "I'd like to believe Ryan wouldn't be so devious, but somehow I can't. I agree with Raven."

"Nothing else really makes sense," Zach admitted. He swore quietly. "So we've probably lost the art."

"We'll get it eventually," Kelsey told him. "Just not this trip."

"The main target was always Ryan," Josh reminded them.

"You weren't supposed to know that," Kelsey said.

Zach gave him a look. "Something I intend to take up with your boss at the first opportunity."

"If you can catch him," Kelsey responded with a grin.

"So where the hell *is* Hagen?"

"He's supposed to be on his way with half a dozen marshals."

"By air?"

"No such luck." Kelsey said, still grinning. "The military isn't real fond of Hagen, and they wouldn't offer *him* a chopper."

Mildly pleased, Josh said, "We're one up on him there."

"And we're on our own," Zach said with a sigh. "And if Ryan has an airlift planned, it'll have to be a helicopter. Army surplus or transport. Nothing else could land around here. We'll have to get him before his ride gets here."

"Easy," Raven said in a solemn tone. "Just stick your head up over the hill, yell something about them being surrounded by the FBI, and accept their surrender."

They stared at Raven in disbelief, and she murmured, "Well, it works in the movies."

"Not without a bloodbath," Zach said dryly. "They have automatic weapons. And, trite though it sounds, Ryan won't be taken alive."

"Sure he will," Teddy said, entering the conversation for the first time.

She was stared at. She stared back.

"The suspense is killing me," Raven murmured.

Teddy grinned at her. "You're married to a commando; do they ever do things the easy way?"

"Not if they can avoid it," Raven answered after careful consideration.

"Thanks a lot," Josh murmured.

"Anytime, darling."

Lucas slid down the hill before anyone could say more. "Ryan just split his forces. Seems to be getting paranoid. Two of his men are heading toward the road."

"That makes it even easier," Teddy said. "It leaves three men, counting Ryan, at the truck. If you guys can take out the two at the road without too much noise—"

"Teddy." Zach was staring at her. "Just what have you got in mind?"

She wasn't about to explain her real motivation—which was to keep Zach out of a gun battle. Nor was she going to admit that she knew very well Zach wanted to kill Ryan; he was no longer on the edge of berserk, but she knew that if there was a battle, neither Ryan nor Zach would stop until one of them was dead.

Teddy didn't know if the others were aware of it, but she could feel the tension in Zach and see the faintly distant, inwardly turned look in his eyes. Light conversation and calm strategy aside, Zach was prowling a deadly inner jungle. She really didn't care one way or the other whether Ryan lived or died, but she didn't want Zach to kill him. Not here. Not now. She wasn't willing to be the cause of another stain on her warrior's soul.

"Teddy?"

She looked at Zach. "The easy way. I have a dart pistol, remember? And enough tranquilizer and darts to give those guys a nice long nap. Within a few yards of them I can get all three before they have time to react."

Several voices responded at once.

"Sounds good."

"The marshals'll *love* sleeping bad guys!"

"Nice and easy."

"No fuss, no bother."

"No way." Zach's voice cut through the rest, and even a stranger would have jumped at the grim note.

Teddy met his stony gaze calmly. "No other way."

"I'll do it," he said in a flat tone.

The others looked at one another and then eased themselves out of the problem. Lucas returned to the top of the hill, Josh and Kelsey went to see about ambushing the two men at the road, and Raven headed for their vehicles to alert Rafferty to the possible approach of an unfriendly helicopter.

Teddy found herself on her feet, wishing dimly that Zach hadn't gotten up also; it was a little difficult for a small woman to look strong and tough when facing a very large one-man army on his feet. But not impossible.

"You're not getting anywhere near Ryan," Zach told her.

"Have you ever handled a dart pistol?"

"I've handled guns."

"Dart pistols are different—or at least mine is—"

"No, Teddy. That bastard's already shot you, kidnapped you, hurt you—"

"All the more reason. I've got a score to settle, too, Zach."

His eyes narrowed. "I'll settle it for you."

She squared her shoulders and met his flinty eyes, her own fierce. "Yes, you would, if I let you. Oh, you'd use my pistol. On two of them. Then the gun would jam—or you'd somehow misplace that third dart—or you'd miss Ryan. Deliberately. Anything to make certain it'll be just you and him."

Something flickered hotly in Zach's eyes. "Teddy—"

"Ever since Ryan . . . took me . . . you've been determined that he'd never see the inside of a jail, haven't you, Zach?"

"Do you know what you're saying?" he asked softly.

"Yes, I know." Her voice became quiet. "Because I'd like to kill him myself. But he's not worth the sleepless nights that would cause me." She was rolling the dice again, gambling that Zach would see that she understood, that she wasn't afraid of him because of the savagery of his intentions. It was very important to her that he see that. Important to them.

She drew a deep breath. "I know how hard it will be for you to let him go, let him live. And if he hadn't taken me, if that wasn't a large part of your reason, I wouldn't try to stop you. But that is why, isn't it, Zach? That's why you don't want to let him go."

Zach was very still, his gaze fixed on her face. "Partly," he finally admitted.

She nodded. "Partly. Because he took something you felt responsible for. Me. The dragon got the lady, and you can't let him get away with that."

For the first time amusement softened the hard line of his mouth. "White charger, rusty armor and all?"

Teddy smiled in return. "Maybe nobody else ever told you, but you were born a few ages too late. And I think I knew that even in the beginning. I think it's why I love you."

This time his entire face softened. Just a little. "Teddy—"

Aware that time was passing, that there were some things they'd have to discuss later, she interrupted. "Even if I thought you loved me, I wouldn't blackmail you emotionally, Zach. If you killed Ryan, it wouldn't change the way I feel about you. Nothing could do that. I'm just asking you to let me do this."

"You're left-handed, and that arm's wounded."

"With guns, I'm actually better right-handed."

After a moment, and in the tone of a final argument, Zach said, "Those guys are pros."

She pulled the dart pistol from her purse and held it firmly. "When it comes to hitting vicious moving animals with this," she said quietly, "I'm a pro."

When the others returned moments later from their errands and approached warily, they found Lucas alone and looking bemused and somewhat stunned.

"Where are they?" Josh asked quickly.

Lucas cleared his throat. "They're circling the clearing to find a better place to use the dart pistol."

"Who's going to—?"

"Teddy. Can you beat that?"

Raven started to smile. "Does that mean what I think it means?"

Her husband drew her close, smiling as well. "All I can say is that I've never—ever—seen Zach back down for anyone. Not with something like this."

"Never underestimate the power," Raven murmured.

"Of women?" Kelsey asked, because he didn't know Zach as well as the others did.

"Of love," Josh told him.

"Oh. That old thing," Kelsey murmured, and followed the others to their vantage point on the hill.

Any old-fashioned dragon slayer would have found the end of the battle something less than rousing, but none of those involved were disappointed. They were all aware that this battle hadn't ended with a whimper but with something quiet and gallant.

Teddy joined Zach in the clearing where not a single weapon had been fired, and both looked at the villain who lay sprawled on his side, snoring softly. Against his will, Zach had to smile.

Looking up at him gravely, Teddy said, "Sometimes the dragon lives. Life's like that."

And after a moment Zach said, "I guess it is, at that."

The semi did indeed hold the shipment of arms, and with the sleeping men bound along with the two others just in case, a brief meeting was held alongside the vehicles.

Lifting a brow at the others, Kelsey said, "My boss kind of figured all of you would be in on the finish. In that event, he said I was to tell you that you'd all be called on to testify if the marshals found you here."

Dryly, Zach said, "He's just avoiding me."

"Of course he is. But it's true, nonetheless."

Nodding, Zach said, "Teddy and I'll take the Porsche, then."

Josh looked at Kelsey. "You can claim the van as being your transportation up here. It's registered in a phony name, anyway—just your style."

"Yeah," Kelsey said blandly, "we federal types do dumb things like that."

Josh ignored that. "The rest of us can hitch a ride out with Rafferty."

They all looked up as—right on cue—the thumping roar of an army helicopter neared. Zach took Teddy's hand, said, "See you back in New York," to the others, and headed off toward Raven's car.

In her husband's ear, Raven said, "Do you think—?"

Josh was watching them leave and said, "I don't know. I've a feeling that fight isn't over yet."

"She's tough," Raven reminded him. "I don't think she'll give up easily."

"I hope not," Josh said. "I hope not."

They drove straight through to Denver, Zach handling the fiery little Porsche with precision. Teddy's bags had been transferred over, and she still didn't know if Zach meant to put her on a plane alone to Boston.

It was late when they arrived in Denver, and the first thing he did was to take her to a doctor. Teddy protested in vain, finally submitting when he calmly promised to have her various wounds checked out if he had to take her to a hospital emergency room. The doctor seemed to know him, asked no questions at all about Teddy's arm or about the state of her wrists. He merely cleaned and bandaged her wounds, gave her a shot to guard against infection, and told Zach to drop in again sometime.

Then they went to a hotel, and Teddy still didn't know what he intended to do. She was afraid to ask.

"A real shower," she said with forced lightness after exploring the roomy suite. Zach was standing by the window, very still; she didn't know if he was with her or not. "Hey, I thought doctors were supposed to report gunshot wounds."

Zach stirred and turned to look at her. "He's a friend. He knew that if it was something he'd need to report, I would have told him."

For a moment Teddy couldn't move. There was something in Zach's eyes that almost broke her heart. "You're going to send me away," she whispered.

"Your sister needs you, remember?" He shrugged out of his jacket and tossed it over a chair, then removed the shoulder holster and placed his gun beside the jacket. His voice was even and calm. "There'll be a car waiting for you in Boston. A replacement for the one I . . . drowned."

"Live with me." Her voice was still, stark. "Let me live with you. Anywhere, it doesn't matter."

"Don't, Teddy."

"Don't what?" Her eyes felt hot, and there was an awful tightness in her chest. "Don't fight for my happiness? I have to, Zach. I love you."

"You'll get over it," he said, very low.

"Will you?"

He crossed the room to her and pulled her into his arms, holding her tightly against him for a long moment. "Don't talk about later," he said finally, roughly. "I don't want to hear about later." When he lifted his head, he was calm, but his eyes were dark and strained.

Teddy drew a deep breath, ignoring the aching tightness around her heart. Pushing him now, she knew, would do nothing except ruin what might well be their last hours together—and she wasn't willing to do that. But she wasn't beaten. Not yet.

"All right." She conjured a smile for him. "Why don't you take a shower while I call room service. We can relax for a while. Can't we?"

They could. For Teddy, it seemed odd to be with Zach with no shadow of danger hanging over them. And when she thought about it, she felt a faint shock at the realization that she had known him less than a week. A lifetime of knowledge and emotions in less than a week.

And yet she didn't feel hurried, confused, or disoriented by the rush of events and feelings. She felt—had felt throughout the past days—that she was standing on a solid base of certainty. She knew what she felt.

A week, a month, a year—it didn't matter. She loved Zach.

Zach knew only too well what was behind the tight feeling in his chest. It had happened before, when he had seen her wound, her blood. When he had heard her scream and known she was in Ryan's cruel hands. His fear for her, the fear of losing her, had gripped his heart like a huge hand, squeezing in agony.

And now he knew he was going to lose her. He would put her on a plane in the morning, bound for Boston and her family and her normal life, in which he wouldn't fit.

She was talkative, stubborn, innately tough, humorous. She had the soft eyes of a doe that would pull things from inside him, things he didn't even know were there; and then those soft eyes turned amber with a cat's enigmatic mystery and lighted fires of need inside him. But hers was a normal life, unshadowed by danger, where the only guns were dart pistols to subdue simple four-legged animals.

His life, his very nature, was shaped by danger. He carried a gun more often than not, and his career was protecting an international corporation, its employees and, particularly, its charismatic leader from the various dangers that were an almost daily occurrence. He talked little, was secretive, stubborn, occasionally explosive.

They were both stubborn—not the best trait to

have in common. But within a very few days something had happened between them. Zach told himself that he knew what it was. Not love but something fleeting, born in difficult and unusual circumstances. Something that would never, could never, last.

Teddy couldn't love him.

Bleakly, he knew it would be worse this time. He was going to lose something he had never lost before, something vitally important to him. And it would be his own action that would send her out of his life. It had to be that way. A clean break while she still looked at him with no fear in her eyes.

Because if he waited, hoped, and then saw that fear, it would tear him apart.

With an effort of will that had never before been so difficult, Zach pushed it all away. He didn't want to think about later. Not now. Only when he had to.

Teddy studied the room-service menu while listening to water running in the bathroom. Zach was shaving first, she realized, and she heard the shower begin as she called room service. She ordered a meal for them but requested that it be sent up in an hour and a half. Then she shed clothing erratically on her way to join Zach in the shower.

The small room was fogged with steam, the glass shower stall a misted barrier between them. Teddy just stood and gazed at him for a moment, intrigued by the hazy outline of his big body as he moved in the stall. And she felt a sudden onrush of her inner storm, sweeping toward her, over her. It was no longer a pain, as it had once been, but the strength and power of it was dizzying.

Need. A hot, gripping need for his touch, his closeness. A driving urge to touch him herself, so forceful that her hands reached out, fumbling, for the shower door without her conscious volition. And when the hot moisture of the stall closed around her, it was as if she had stepped bodily into the center of that surging tropical storm.

Zach turned, his eyes sweeping over her. "You'll get the bandages wet," he murmured.

"You're a smart man—I'm sure you'll think of something." Her voice was husky.

He stepped closer, easing her body against his, and his mouth covered hers in a deep, possessive kiss. "What I'm thinking of right now," he said against her lips, "isn't bandages."

But he did think of them, of course. One bandage covered her left arm from elbow to shoulder, and both wrists were bound. Which meant that it was almost impossible to keep them all dry. Almost impossible.

Being a man of many talents, Zach managed the impossible. He used his own large body to keep the majority of the spray off her, yet even managed to wash her hair. He was in an unusual mood, she thought fleetingly, teasing, laughing softly. His eyes clear but dark and curiously still. He handled her body with familiarity, and yet she had the feeling that he was . . . memorizing her. It made her throat ache.

Astonishingly, when they emerged from the shower stall, her bandages were still dry.

But the king-size bed got quite damp, because neither of them wanted to waste time with towels.

Room service came and went; darkness fell outside. Room service came and went again. They dressed in the absolute minimum to answer the door but otherwise remained naked and in bed. And they made love. Just as the days before had intensified their time together, so did these hours intensify their loving.

With every instinct she could claim, Teddy knew that Zach cared for her, but she knew also that he intended to send her away, out of his life. He wouldn't even wait, give them a chance, and she knew why.

A single lamp by the bed provided the only light, and it was late when Teddy stirred at his side and lifted her head. She was on her stomach beside him, the covers drawn up to his waist and over her hips. She looked at him for a long time, knowing that he was awake, even though his eyes were closed. It had been a long day, with a sleepless night before that for him, yet neither of them could sleep.

And Teddy was racking her brain, trying desperately to come up with something that would convince him how sure her feelings were. "Zach? If—if you did believe I loved you, would there be a place in your life for me?"

He opened his eyes, and one hand began toying with her vivid hair. "Let it go, honey," he murmured.

"I could never be afraid of you."

"Teddy—"

With everything inside her tight, her voice emerged tense and strained. "Has it occurred to you that I've thrown away every shred of pride I've got? I've never done that, Zach. But I don't care. Just give us a month, can you do that? And if after that you want me to go—"

"No," he said softly, closing his eyes again. "I can't do that, Teddy."

"For my sake or yours?"

"Both. For both of us."

She traced the scar over his ribs with trembling fingers. Quietly, despairingly, she said, "You're afraid of something that's never going to happen. I'll stop breathing before I stop loving you."

Zach had never wanted anything in his life more than he wanted to believe her. But he was locked inside himself, alone in the way he'd always been alone, and the only thing to keep him company there was the cold dread he felt at losing her.

He pulled her closer to his side, keeping his eyes closed because he didn't know what she might see in them. And he felt her lips feathering along the scar on his cheek.

"You said I belonged to you," she whispered.

"For a while," he said. "Just for a while."

Teddy scooted down and rested her cheek on his chest, staring with burning eyes and seeing only an emptiness inside her. He was going to send her away. And she was going to go. Only the passage of time would convince him, if even that would. She didn't know if she'd be able to stand it. But she wasn't ready to give up entirely, not yet. Not while the faintest hope remained.

Teddy awoke in the pre-dawn hours, conscious of twinges low down in her stomach. She wasn't aware of the significance of that at first, merely uncomfortable and restless. When she did realize, she crept silently from the bed, leaving Zach sleeping deeply.

In the darkness she gathered what she needed from her luggage and went into the bathroom, closing the door behind her softly and turning on the light.

And she hadn't realized until then just how much she had hoped. She had nothing to lessen the growing pain of cramps but wouldn't have taken aspirin even if she'd had it.

It should hurt, she thought. It should hurt to know she wasn't carrying Zach's child.

The sun was well up when Zach awoke, and he was instantly aware that he was alone in the bed. He half sat up even as his eyes opened, then relaxed as he saw her. She was in a chair by the window, fully dressed, sitting with both legs over the arm of the chair, gazing at nothing.

She was pale and still and seemed to be in a world of her own. And even as he watched, a tear emerged from the corner of one eye and trailed down her cheek, silvery in the sunlight.

"Teddy?"

She looked at him, turning her head slowly. "You haven't changed your mind?" Her voice almost wasn't there.

"No."

Teddy nodded a little, unsurprised. "Well, you won't have to worry about—about repercussions, Zach. I am definitely not pregnant."

Zach didn't put a name to what he felt in that moment. But he dimly wondered how it was possible to feel so empty, so much like a hollowed out shell.

Nine

Both of Teddy's parents were at her sister's house in Boston when she arrived there. They were an affectionate family and a talkative one, except for her father, so there was much exclaiming for a while. In particular, much speculation took place over the brand-new, gleaming blue Impala Teddy had arrived driving. But she wasn't ready to tell them that story, and after a while her shrewd family stopped pressing.

Jenny, who looked enough like Teddy to be her twin, seemed somewhat relieved at stepping temporarily from the focus of family concern; after two miscarriages and five hazardous months of holding on to the life she carried, she confided to Teddy that she was a bit tired of being wrapped in cotton wool—especially since this time she *knew* her baby would be safely born.

Teddy didn't doubt that knowledge, particularly when Jenny told her of having "seen" her daughter toddling around on strong legs.

As for herself, Teddy assumed a calm, if not cheerful, expression; assured her red-haired mother that she was fine; hugged her tall, laconic, silver-haired father; and brought her bags into her sister's warm, cheerful house. Her brother-in-law had been forced to take a business trip, which was why his in-laws were watching over his wife, and so Teddy was spared his sharp eye; even after four years of marriage Robert wasn't yet accustomed to the Tylers' laid-back affection for one another and tended to be somewhat persistent in his own anxious concern.

For three days her family was careful not to pressure her. Then, on the fourth day, her father went in search of her. She was in the back garden, absently watching the yard across the way where children built a snowman, more of the white stuff falling all around them.

"Teddy?"

She roused herself and turned to look up at her father. "Hi, Daddy. You didn't have to come out. You could have yelled."

"I never yell."

Teddy smiled a little. "No. You never do. I guess some people are just born that way."

Justin Tyler leaned against a bare lower branch of a tree they were under and joined her in contemplating the falling snow. In an incurious tone he asked, "You've met someone recently who wasn't born that way?"

She understood that her father was willing to listen, if she was prepared now to talk. And since his wise counsel had eased many a path through her life, she decided that she did indeed want to talk. And the nicest thing about her father was that he was amazingly adept at reading between the lines.

"Oh, not really. He doesn't yell. He can be very cold

when he's angry, but it takes a lot to anger him. And when he's pushed too far—I mean, really too far—then he just goes deadly quiet. Like a ticking bomb."

"Did he explode?" her father asked idly.

"No. I stopped him," she explained simply.

Justin Tyler glanced at his daughter. "I see. And if you hadn't stopped him?"

"I think he would have killed a man. A very bad man." She looked up at her father's expressionless face, suddenly anxious that he understand. "The man tried to use me as a tool, to force Zach to do as he wanted, and he hurt me." Absently, she rubbed her left arm, an action her father's quick glance took note of. "Zach didn't like that."

Blessedly unconcerned regarding the circumstances of all this, Justin merely nodded. "Understandable."

She smiled a little at the laconic comment. "You've met him, Daddy. Zach Steele. He works for—"

"Josh Long. Yes, I remember. Quite an impressive man."

"He's a good man, Daddy."

"Of course he is, darling, or you wouldn't be in love with him."

Teddy felt quick, hot tears start to her eyes. "He sent me away. But I know he cares about me. I *know* it. He just won't believe that I love him. Daddy—I saw—I saw him with me. At least, I think I did. And I saw all the jungles he's fought in, and the dangers."

Her father put an arm around her shoulders and hugged her. "Then give it a little time," he advised. And because he had, after all, married one of those determined, red-haired, myopic, left-handed ladies and raised two more, he added softly, "If you stopped him from killing a man, I expect you'll be able to stop him from walking out of your life. One way or another."

Very conscious of the tearing pain of loving Zach and not being with him, Teddy nonetheless felt her wavering courage steady. Of course. Of course she would.

One way or another.

Zach had never before been overly conscious of the passing of time. Living an active life as he did, his time was generally full and satisfying. But not now.

He walked on the beach, letting the steady surging of the ocean seep into his body, feeling the salt spray on his face. He had argued with himself again and again as days turned into weeks, telling himself that she would know by now, that he could just visit to see if she was all right.

Except that he couldn't do that.

He felt suspended, numb. The only emotion not encased in that numbness was fear, and he was distantly surprised by that. It was an emotion he'd only become familiar with recently . . . since he'd met Teddy. And since then it seemed a constant part of him, a small, cold lump of ice inside him.

And it was that which kept him walking the beach for hours, numb and alone. That cold lump that rose up inside his throat when he thought of seeing her again. He wanted to see her again, hold her, love her. Dear God, he wanted that. In less than a week she'd changed his life so much that being without her was almost intolerable.

He thought he'd survive this, if not entirely whole,

then at least scarred only inside where no one would see. But those scars weren't the simple ones of the flesh that would heal, then hurt no more. These scars, he knew, would ache for the rest of his life.

What he had once felt for that other woman was nothing compared to this. He had never felt love before, he knew that now. And that was why he was so afraid to see Teddy again.

Seeing fear and wariness in her eyes was something he'd never survive.

Lucas Kendrick was just hanging up the phone when his boss walked unannounced into his office, and he looked up to say in a more or less automatic tone, "Anybody'd think you worked here."

Josh didn't bother to respond to the remark, perfectly aware that his men were as comfortable as he with his habit of going in search of them when needed; he rarely summoned anyone to his own office. Resting a hip on the corner of the desk, he asked, "Have you found him?"

"Yes." Rather than pleased, Lucas looked worried. "He hasn't done a damned thing to stop anyone from finding him. It's as if he just doesn't care. I've *never* known a time when Zach didn't take precautions as habitually as breathing, especially during the last five years or so because we've all made enemies. Airline tickets, hotel, rental car—all in his own name and obtained with his own credit cards. He couldn't have left a broader trail if he'd marked it on a map."

Josh sighed a little. It had been he who had insisted that Zach take a real vacation, because he had known that his friend needed time to himself. But that had been three weeks ago, and Josh had grown worried. "Where is he?" he asked Lucas.

"Right where we should have expected him to be," Lucas replied with a grunt. "At the Oregon house."

The lonely, cliff-hugging aerie on the coast of Oregon belonged to Long Enterprises, but Josh rarely visited himself; he and Raven preferred their lodge in the Catskills. So the Oregon house had become a retreat for Josh's friends, offered for their use whenever they wanted. The agents who looked after the house had standing orders to admit any of the company's executives without question or comment, and the house was generally occupied throughout the year.

"I'll call—" Josh began.

"I just tried." Lucas shook his head. "He's not answering the phone. But the agents say he's there and has been all along. They've restocked the supplies each week as usual, so at least he's eating."

"All right. We'll leave him alone a while longer."

In a tone that was almost angry Lucas said, "Anybody could see that girl was in love with him. Why the hell doesn't he go after her instead of hiding out alone like a gut-shot bear?"

Josh could have told him but didn't. Instead, he silently agreed with something Lucas had said. Zach *was* like a wounded animal, going off alone to heal himself—or die. And only the knowledge that he could do absolutely nothing to help his friend kept Josh from ordering his Lear readied so he could fly out there and confront him.

The intercom system buzzed a summons, and Lucas answered impatiently. "What is it, Jackie?"

"There's someone waiting for Mr. Long in his office," Lucas's secretary reported.

Lucas looked up at Josh, then directed a second question at the speaker. "Who is it?"

"A Miss Tyler."

When Josh entered his huge office a few moments later, he immediately saw Teddy standing to the right of his desk as she stared out at the breathtaking view of the city afforded by floor-to-ceiling glass. She was dressed with casual elegance in a smoke-colored silk dress, her vibrant hair piled atop her head and high heels lending her height.

She didn't turn to look at him, but her profile was revealed as he slowly approached, and Josh could see that this was not the fierce, intrepid, and somewhat disheveled young woman who had thrown herself between Zach and a bloody mortal war.

This Teddy, he realized with a jolt, had walked through some inner fire and emerged whole but scarred. She was a fraction thinner, and though she looked more fragile than before, it was the deceptive, seeming fragility of a diamond born in the dark, relentless pressures of unmeasured depths. And though there were no new lines on her face, something in the stillness of her eyes whispered of some dreadful pain endured.

"He's not coming after me, is he?" she asked quietly when Josh reached her side.

"I don't think so," Josh responded just as quietly and without hesitation.

"You've known him longer than anyone. Tell me something honestly?"

"Of course."

"Is it because he doesn't care?"

"Because he cares too much."

She looked at him then, a faint, indomitable smile curving her lips. "Then I'll just have to go after him, won't I?"

Josh looked at her for a long moment, smiling a little himself. Then he stepped to his desk and lifted the phone, asking that his Lear be readied for a flight to Oregon.

"He's there?"

"Yes."

"Josh, you don't have to lend me the jet—"

"I know, but I want to help. I love him, too, you know."

"Yes," she said. "I know."

The rental car Josh had arranged for her was waiting at the airport in Portland, and Teddy followed the directions she'd been given to reach the house where Zach was staying alone. It was a fairly long drive for a woman in Teddy's impatient, anxious frame of mind, but she endured it. She'd gotten good these past weeks at enduring what she had to.

It was late afternoon when she finally negotiated the long, winding drive up to the house. At the top of the drive, scant yards from the cliff rising above the Pacific, the house blended perfectly with the tall trees all around it. It was an A-frame built of cedar and glass, appearing both rough and elegant at the same time.

Teddy parked her car near the sedan Zach had rented, leaving her bags as she went up the gravel walk to the front door. She started to knock, then squared her shoulders and used the key Josh had given her, opening the door and going inside.

And she didn't have to call his name to know that Zach wasn't in the house. She explored methodically, a distant part of her mind approving the spaciousness of the ground floor that was basically all one room, and the loft above that contained three bedrooms. And the only indications that Zach had used one bedroom were the clothes folded neatly in drawers and hanging in the closet, and the shaving kit tucked away in the bathroom; otherwise, it was as neat as if no one slept there.

Teddy went back downstairs, through the living area with its deep carpet and comfortable furniture, through the kitchen that was separated from the main room by a waist-high partition, and out the back door. She went to the edge of the cliff, some instinct guiding her, and when she looked at the narrow strip of beach far below, she saw him.

He was standing utterly still, gazing out over the ocean, hands in the pockets of his jeans. He was alone. He looked alone.

He looked lonely.

After a moment Teddy went back to the house. She returned to her car, got her bags, and carried them into the house. Then she unpacked. In Zach's bedroom.

Burning her bridges.

She was sitting, waiting, halfway down the spiral stairway when he returned more than an hour later. She didn't call attention to herself with any sound but just watched as he crossed the living area and knelt to build a fire in the stone fireplace. His every movement was as graceful as she remembered, as riveting, and she watched him with hungry eyes.

He rose finally, and she did as well, moving silently across the thick carpet until she was a few feet behind him. He was standing with head bent, gazing into the fire, and she could only hope that it was thoughts of her that seemed to have blunted his jungle-bred awareness of his surroundings.

"Zach?"

He stiffened, his shoulders hunching as though guarding against a blow. He didn't make a sound or turn to face her.

Teddy took a deep, silent breath and spoke quietly. "A funny thing happened when I started east a few weeks ago. My car died on the side of a mountain, and I met a dangerous man. I was suddenly in the middle of a lot of things I hadn't planned on. There were criminals and guns and stolen art. There were feelings I'd never known before. Everything happened—fast.

"And then that dangerous man sent me away. He said I'd get over it, what I felt. He said it wasn't real. And I'd never felt like that before, so he could have been right. Because of that, I left. I wanted to be sure. For his sake as well as my own."

After a long moment she finished in a fierce tone, "Zach, dammit, I didn't come three thousand miles to tell you that you were *right!*"

Still, he refused to look at her. He was standing stiffly, utterly motionless, and she realized that he was afraid to look in her eyes. Afraid of what he might see there. She stepped closer, still behind him, all her energy bent on reaching him.

Chaining her own inner wildness, she said in a deliberately stony voice, "I have never in my life met such a stubborn man, Zach Steele. Did you really think I'd believe all that garbage about chemistry and biology and lust? Did you really think I'd meekly allow myself to be sent out of your life for my own good? Oh, I went away. Because I knew you had to be sure. Because I knew damned well there was no other way of convincing you."

She thought she could hear him breathing now, a rough, uneven sound, and pressed on in a voice that was beginning to reflect the wildness inside her. "What makes you think you're so damned hard to love, Zach? It was the easiest thing I've ever done to fall in love with you. So easy. It would have happened no matter where we were. In a cabin, on a boat, in a desert, or in the middle of Times Square at high noon!"

She tried to swallow the lump in her throat. "Do you know what was hard, Zach? Not being with you. Waking up alone in the morning. Drinking my lousy coffee instead of that wonderful stuff you make. That was hard. That was harder than anything.

"Maybe it won't be so easy to live with a tough, dangerous man. Because you can't turn away from danger and you won't willingly take me with you into any more jungles. And we'll probably fight about that. We'll probably fight about these uncontrollable macho instincts of yours and—and your secretive nature. You don't talk much and I talk all the time, but—but you can always shut me up if you want to. You . . . know how to do that.

"Zach, what I'm trying to say is that living with you in jungles or cities or deserts or anywhere could never be harder than living without you."

Teddy wasn't aware that she was crying, or that her nails were biting into her palms. "And I'm not leaving you again," she told him intensely. "Never again, do you hear me, Zach?" She caught her breath, whispering finally, "Unless you can tell me that you didn't come after me because you didn't want to, because you didn't care enough. Can you tell me that, Zach?"

"No." It was a grinding sound, raw and hoarse. "No, I can't tell you that." He turned slowly toward her, and what he saw in her eyes drained the tension from his strained face. His hands lifted, framing her face, his thumbs brushing away her tears. "What have I done to you?" he asked huskily.

"You sent me away," she whispered. "Don't ever do that again."

And then she was in his arms, held in a fiercely tender embrace, and Zach's broken voice was muffled against her neck. "I love you. God, honey, I love you so much! I don't think I could have stood it much longer."

She could hear the desolation in his voice, the strain of emotions held under control for far too long, and everything inside her opened up to him.

"Love me," she whispered, and the storm inside her raged when Zach guided her down to the deep carpet before the fireplace.

Cradled in his arms, she said curiously, "Would you have come after me?"

"I was scared to death even thinking about it," he confessed, his deep voice a rumble. "But I would have. My head was telling me you couldn't possibly really love me, but I couldn't stand not knowing for sure. I would have had to find out, even though I was afraid my head was right."

Teddy raised herself on an elbow and smiled down at him. "Are you always so stubborn?" she asked.

"Yes. Daunting, isn't it?"

"I'm terrified," she said solemnly. "And I think there are still a few battles left to be fought."

Zach opened his eyes and peered at her warily. "Uh-huh. You mentioned a few earlier, if I remember. Do you think we might postpone the war, though? At least until after I talk you into marrying me?"

She tilted her head thoughtfully. "Was that a proposal?" she asked, uninterested in wars.

"The beginning of one."

"Well, finish it."

"My beautiful love—"

"Yes. I'll marry you."

He smiled slowly, and his eyes were dark and deep. "I love you, Teddy. I'll spend the rest of my life proving that to you."

Gently, she said, "Just spend the rest of your life *with* me, Zach."

Pulling her toward him, he murmured just before his lips met hers, "I'll never do anything easier than that."

Epilogue

In his cramped office where he rarely worked, Kelsey
tucked in his elbows and typed disgustedly. "You'd
better be glad Zach found himself a lady," he advised his boss in a voice that was trying to assume
the rhythm of his typing. "Otherwise, if he hadn't
been so distracted, he'd have been out for your blood.
Damn. I typed *blood*."

The office had no window, so Hagen gazed out the
door, flapping his hands gently behind his back.
The portrait of a man deep in thought.

Kelsey wasn't impressed. "Why don't you give it
up, boss? You've got a snowball's chance in hell of
snaring Lucas for an assignment, and even if you
manage it, you'll just be giving Zach another opportunity to clean your clock."

Hagen turned and stared at him. "Clean my clock?"
he inquired with awful dignity.

Still not impressed, Kelsey said, "Put your lights
out. Ring your bell. Beat hell out of you. Take your
choice."

Pulling a folded paper from his pocket, Hagen opened it and studied the closely spaced type. After a moment he said musingly, "Skeletons in the closet."

Kelsey stopped typing and leaned back as far as he was able. His lean face was unusually grim. "I hope you don't mean what I think you mean. Because if you've stumbled over some dark secret and plan to blackmail Lucas—"

"That's a dirty word, my boy."

"It sure as hell is."

Hagen's Cupid's-bow lips curved in a smile, and his twinkling little eyes were brighter than usual. "And unnecessary, I assure you. Kendrick will take the assignment, if only to complete the job his friend started. No, the skeletons in the closet are something else entirely. The human element."

Kelsey rolled his eyes toward the ceiling. "Don't tell me. You're going to partner Lucas with someone out of his dark and stormy past?"

Hagen looked at the paper he held again, his expression thoughtful. "Dark, certainly. Stormy? I don't know. He seems to have covered his tracks well."

Beginning to be seriously alarmed, Kelsey said, "Boss, if you rake up something he wants to forget, you'd better be ready to tangle with all of those guys who work for Josh. And you don't want that."

He was splendidly ignored. "The human element," Hagen murmured to himself. "Yes. This should do it."

Kelsey groaned.

THE EDITOR'S CORNER

One of the best "presents" I've received at Bantam is the help of the very talented and wonderfully enthusiastic Barbara Alpert, who has written the copy for the back cover of almost every LOVESWEPT romance since the first book. (In fact, only three in all this time haven't been written by Barbara, and I wrote those.) As usual, Barbara has done a superb job of showcasing all the books next month, and so I thought I would give you a sneak peek at her copy on the marvelous books you can expect to keep your holiday spirits high.

First, we are delighted to welcome a brand-new writer—and our first Canadian author—Judy Gill, with **HEAD OVER HEELS,** LOVESWEPT #228. "The sultry laughter and tantalizing aromas that wafted across the fence from next door were enough to make a grown man cry, Buck Halloran thought—or else climb eight-foot fences! But the renowned mountain climber was confined to a wheelchair, casts on one arm and one leg ... how could he meet the woman behind the smoky voice, the temptress who was keeper of the goodies? ... He had to touch her, searing her lips with kisses that seduced her heart and soul—and Darcy Gallagher surrendered to the potent magic of his embrace. But the handsome wanderer who whispered sexy promises to her across the hedge at midnight had his eyes on a higher mountain, a new adventure, while she yearned to make a home for children and the man she loved. Could they join their lives and somehow share the dreams that gave them joy?"

Sandra Brown has given us a memorable gift of love in **TIDINGS OF GREAT JOY,** LOVESWEPT #229. As Barbara describes it, "Ria Lavender hadn't planned on spending a passionate Christmas night in front of a roaring fire with Taylor Mackensie. But somehow the scents of pine tree, wood smoke, and male flesh produced a kind of spontaneous combustion inside her, and morning found the lovely architect lying on her silver fox coat beside the mayor-elect, a man she hardly knew. Ten weeks later she knew she was pregnant with Taylor's child ... and insisted they had to marry. A marriage 'in name only,' she promised him. Taylor agreed to a wedding, but shocked Ria with his demand that they live together as husband and wife—in every way. She couldn't deny she wanted him, the lady-killer with the devil's grin, but

(continued)

there was danger in succumbing to the heat he roused—in falling for a man she couldn't keep."

Prepare yourself for a session of hearty laughter and richly warming emotion when you read Joan Elliott Pickart's **ILLUSIONS,** LOVESWEPT #230. Barbara teases you unmercifully with her summary of this one! "There was definitely a naked man asleep in Cassidy Cole's bathtub! With his ruggedly handsome face and 'kissin' lips,' Sagan Jones was a single woman's dream, and how could she resist a smooth-talking vagabond with roving hands who promised he'd stay only until his luggage caught up with him? Sagan had come to Cherokee, Arizona, after promising Cassidy's brother he'd check up on her. He'd flexed his muscles, smiled his heart-stopping smile, and won over everyone in town except her. . . . Sagan had spent years running from loneliness, and though his lips vowed endless pleasures, Cassidy knew he wasn't a man to put down roots. . . . Could she make him see that in a world full of mirages and dreams that died with day, her love was real and everlasting?"

Hagen strikes again in Kay Hooper's delightful **THE FALL OF LUCAS KENDRICK,** LOVESWEPT #231. As Barbara tells you, "Time was supposed to obscure memories, but when Kyle Griffon saw the sunlight glinting off Lucas Kendrick's hair, she knew she'd never stopped waiting for him. Ten years before, he'd awakened her woman's passion, and when he left without a word, her quicksilver laughter had turned to anger, and her rebel's heart to a wild flirtation with danger—anything to forget the pain of losing him. Now he was back, and he needed her help in a desperate plan— but did she dare revive the flame of desire that once had burned her?" Only Josh, Raven, Rafferty, a few other fictional characters, Kay, Barbara, and I know right now. Be sure that you're one of the first next month to get the answer!

You can have the wish you wish as you read this: another great love story from Iris Johansen who gives you **STAR LIGHT, STAR BRIGHT,** LOVESWEPT #232. "When the golden-haired rogue in the black leather jacket dodged a barrage of bullets to rescue her, Quenby Swenson thrilled . . . with fear and with excitement," says Barbara most accurately. "Gunner Nilsen had risked his life to save her, but when he promised to cherish her for a lifetime, she refused to believe him. And yet she knew somehow he'd

(continued)

never lie to her, never hurt her, never leave her—even though she hardly knew him at all. He shattered her serenity, rippled her waters, vowing to play her body like the strings of a harp . . . until he'd learned all the melodies inside her. Quenby felt her heart swell with yearning for the dreams Gunner wove with words and caresses. Did she dare surrender to this mysterious man of danger, the untamed lover who promised her their souls were entwined for all time?"

For one of the most original, whimsical, and moving romances ever, you can't beat **THE BARON**, LOVESWEPT #233 by Sally Goldenbaum. Barbara whets your appetite with this terrific description: "Disguised as a glittering contessa for a glamorous mystery weekend, Hallie Finnegan knew anything was possible—even being swept into the arms of a dashing baron! She'd never been intriguing before, never enchanted a worldly man who stunned her senses with hungry kisses beneath a full moon. Once the 'let's pretend mystery' was solved, though, they shed their costumes, revealing Hallie for the shy librarian with freckles she was—but wealthy, elegant Nick Harrington was still the baron . . . and not in her league. When Nick turned up on her doorstep in pursuit of his fantasy lady, Hallie was sure he'd discover his mistake and run for the hills!"

It's a joy for me to send you the same heartfelt wishes for the season that we've sent you every year since LOVESWEPT began. May your New Year be filled with all the best things in life—the company of good friends and family, peace and prosperity, and of course, love.

Warm wishes for 1988 from all of us at LOVESWEPT.

Sincerely,

Carolyn Nichols

Carolyn Nichols
  Editor

LOVESWEPT
Bantam Books, Inc.
666 Fifth Avenue
New York, NY 10103